P9-DNL-532

THE GAY PHOENIX

Also by Michael Innes

THE APPLEBY FILE
THE MYSTERIOUS COMMISSION
APPLEBY'S OTHER STORY
APPLEBY'S ANSWER
THE OPEN HOUSE
AN AWKWARD LIE
DEATH AT THE CHASE
PICTURE OF GUILT
A CHANGE OF HEIR
THE BLOODY WOOD
APPLEBY INTERVENES
MONEY FROM HOLME
THE CRABTREE AFFAIR
SILENCE OBSERVED
THE CASE OF SONIA WAYWARD
HARE SETTING UP
THE LONG FAREWELL
APPLEBY TALKS AGAIN
DEATH ON A QUIET DAY
A QUESTION OF QUEENS
THE MAN FROM THE SEA
DEAD MAN'S SHOES
CHRISTMAS AT CANDLESHOE
ONE-MAN SHOW
THE PAPER THUNDERBOLT
THE CASE OF THE JOURNEYING BOY
A NIGHT OF ERRORS
DEATH BY WATER

The Gay Phoenix

A RED BADGE NOVEL OF SUSPENSE

Michael Innes

DODD, MEAD & COMPANY
NEW YORK

THE JEFFERSON-MADISON REGIONAL PUBLIC LIBRARY CHARLOTTESVILLE, VIRGINIA

Copyright © J. I. M. Stewart 1976
All rights reserved
No part of this book may be reproduced in any form
without permission in writing from the publisher
First published in the United States 1977

1 2 3 4 5 6 7 8 9 10

ISBN: 0-396-07442-1
Library of Congress Catalog Card Number: 77-74674
Printed in the United States of America

M
Innes
cop. 1

CONTENTS

PROLOGUE

Sundry Persons at Sea

I

THE POVEY BROTHERS eyed one another. Charles Povey's gaze was more fixed than Arthur Povey's—which was in the nature of things, since Charles was dead. Arthur found he greatly disliked being stared at by a corpse. As with Banquo's ghost when it had obeyed Macbeth's summons to the feast, there was no speculation in the eyes that it did glare with. But there was no reason for Arthur to suppose that there was anything particularly unusual about his feelings. Most people probably found such an experience disagreeable, and that was why it was customary to close the eyes of deceased persons. You put out a finger—Arthur Povey supposed—and edged down first one lid and then the other, rather as if coping with some defect in the mechanism of a 'sleeping' doll.

For some moments, Arthur found he lacked courage to perform this office for Charles. He sat back and imagined —for he had a lively imagination—a fly crawling slowly across first his brother's right eye and then his brother's left eye : sightless and unflinching orbs. Not that there could be many flies around. Not here aboard a small craft tossing uneasily in the middle of the Pacific Ocean.

And Charles—Arthur reflected with what was only a fresh spurt of familiar resentment—had died abruptly and for no good reason at all. He had simply not hopped out of the way quick enough. And as a consequence of his lethargic behaviour his younger brother had been left in a more desperate hole than ever. It was absolutely *like* Charles to fix things that way.

Still, one had to be fair. Arthur's hole, with Charles dead,

9

was not quite so desperate as Charles's hole would have been, had it been Arthur who had incontinently got himself killed. This was because it was Arthur who really knew the sea. That was why he had been dragged into this 'adventure' in the first place. Charles had recruited him without ceremony, and in exchange for nothing more than his keep, precisely as if he had been some adequately qualified lounger of the sort to be picked up on any water-front. Damn Charles and his adventures. They had always been idiotic and gratuitous. There wasn't even money in them.

Not that this one had looked particularly hazardous. The yacht had been—it still mostly was—uncommonly well-found. You could advertise it in a journal for freshwater sailors as owning all mod cons. It was true that—now, and since the sizeable storm which had just blown itself out—the yacht lacked one or two rather important bits and pieces. Notably, it lacked its main-mast. That was what Charles had failed to get out of the way of as it came crashing down—with the consequence that the up-flying butt of the thing, lethally jagged, had gone through the back of his head like a knife. The moment had been one of sheer nightmare—particularly as Arthur's own head hadn't escaped scot-free. Something, he didn't know quite what, had given it a flip or blip which had landed him with a filthy headache now.

Cautiously, and for the third or fourth time, Arthur Povey felt his skull. You could fracture your skull, he supposed, without its then positively wobbling under your fingers. But there couldn't be so much as a cut on his, since with the slightest scalp-wound you bled like a pig. And he certainly wasn't concussed. So he had been lucky. Lucky so far.

As for the yacht, he could continue to make do with it. Once back in a trade-route, his job would be simply not to fall fatally asleep in the path of an unstoppable tanker before hailing something more likely to be charitably interested in him. Eventually he would collect a certain amount of credit and publicity (but not, unfortunately, remunerative publicity) for managing to turn up alive. Of course, a Sunday paper might buy his 'story'. There would be a small something in that.

Hunched by the idle wheel, Arthur Povey brooded. Alone on a wide wide sea, he brooded for a long time. Not that he was unconscious of some action as being required of him fairly quickly. The bloody sun at noon—and here his sole working capital, his imagination, was at work again—would very soon operate on his brother's body in an undesirable way. The sun breeds maggots in a dead dog, being a god kissing carrion. (Or a good kissing-carrion, Arthur crazily told himself—recalling some fragment of his expensive and useless education.) Hygiene called for the rapid disposal of Charles. Decency and piety required the rummaging out of some scrap of sail-cloth and the stitching of the body into it before consignment to the deep. There was even something in the Book of Common Prayer that one ought to read aloud first. (The Poveys were English gentlemen, and had been well brought up.) It seemed doubtful, however, whether the mod cons ran to such a volume. Nautical manuals and a few mildly erotic paperbacks constituted, so far as he could remember, the entire library the *Gay Phoenix* boasted.

Arthur Povey scowled. The contracting of his forehead brought on an extra stab of pain, and again his fingers went to the back of his head—to the spot which, on his brother's head, he didn't propose, if he could help it, to look at again. A less uncultivated man than Charles, he was always irritated when he remembered that Charles's trim craft bore that peculiarly idiotic name. The *Gay Phoenix*! There had been a time when Charles had indulged a rich man's fancy for owning race-horses, and it seemed to be a convention that you could call such brutes any nonsensical thing you pleased. Yachts ought to be different. Arthur Povey, being a person of exact sensibility, was very clear about that.

This trivial displeasure was scarcely one to take up much time, and he was therefore startled when he suddenly noticed what was happening to the now swiftly moderating sea. That vast unharvested deep had taken to sliding up to and beneath the *Gay Phoenix* in a tumble of molten golden guineas—a perfectly familiar phenomenon, but one declaring that the sun had dropped almost to the horizon. He had been sitting immobile and paralysed for hours! The discovery frightened him. It frightened him because it told him he *was* frightened; that shock had been succeeded by blind terror. *Charles had died.* Charles had suffered death by misadventure—something the possibility of which one was always theoretically aware of, but the actual enactment of which before one's eyes appeared a brute and incredible thing. It was, after a fashion, a natural death, yet it now seemed unnatural in the highest degree: a stroke so arbitrary as to induce ungovernable fear when one tried to focus it. Why had the Dark Angel chosen Charles? Equally it might have chosen him! He felt like a man who had been playing Russian roulette with a revolver every second chamber of which held a live bullet. He had pulled the trigger and there had been nothing but a click. The issue might have been a shattering oblivion.

But he was also paralysed like this because he was in the grip of two contradictory impulses before the problem of Charles's body. He loathed it—so that he wanted to jump up, seize it cruelly by the heels, and pitch it without more ado to the sharks. At the same time, he couldn't bear even to think of parting with it. Inert matter though it was, it yet seemed all that was left to him of the breathing world. With Charles gone, loneliness would be his sole companion.

Yet these were unmanly thoughts and emotions. They just wouldn't do. Arthur Povey managed to take a deep breath. *His* lungs were still in working order. It was his duty to keep them that way. It was even his duty to find them, if possible, a larger air. In life, his brother Charles had been disposed to do precious little for him. Could Charles—the speculation began to stir dimly in his numbed brain—be made to do rather more for him in death?

The headache was going away, and the relief of this was immense. Only, he had an odd sensation as if what he was thus parting with had owned some physical dimension within his skull, in which there was now as a consequence a small vacant space waiting to be filled up with something else. He wondered whether he had suffered some mild concussion after all. Fleetingly he was aware of the vague visual image of a football-field, and of a boy—who might be himself— scrambling out of a messy confusion of flailing limbs and wandering round in disconcerting circles until led off to the pavilion. He wondered whether, if set in the middle of a large open space now, he would begin to behave in this way. What had thus drifted into his mind so inconsequently had the feel of a memory rather than of a random creation of the mind, yet he could provide it with no context in his own experience. For some minutes after the picture faded, he continued to be unreasonably worried by this. He had to pull himself together in order to take hold of his present situation.

A spectator—but even the Dark Angel had departed— might have found something a shade macabre in the first action that Arthur Povey then bestirred himself to perform. His brother's body was lightly clad in shorts and a singlet, and there were only plimsolls on his feet. Arthur stripped off the lot and threw everything into the sea. The small operation was surprisingly difficult. Charles's limbs were like those of a sulky and unco-operative child, resentful of being undressed and put to bed. For a full minute Arthur stood panting slightly, his own legs, braced and sentient, responding to the sway of the yacht. The body thus spoiled was lean, strong, strangely young. It ought obviously to have

13

gone on living for years and years—as he himself, by two years Charles's junior, would certainly do.

A wave thudded, and the dead man helplessly lurched a little against the bulwark. Even so, it was without indignity. Arthur looked at his brother's broad shoulders and narrow hips, at his flat belly, the fine hairs glinting golden on his chest, the dark curled abundant hair below. Charles had been a proper man. But Arthur himself, for that matter, was a proper man too. They were alike in physique and features, although they had not been very alike in temperament or in the course of their lives. Beset by a sudden irrational doubt, and still reluctant to raise that head and accept the verdict it gave, Arthur put a hand on Charles's heart. It was still, and the body it had served was cold. He let his living right hand touch Charles's dead left hand—and for a moment pause there, as if some message had been transmitted to him. He felt down Charles's side : the taut rib-cage, the hollow thigh, the moulded knee. Charles's sex, exposed before him in a manner suggesting the drunkenness of Noah, made him momentarily frown. He hadn't known much about that part of his brother's life.

He began to think about what he did know—both in this regard and others. His mind moved into the past—but gropingly, as if even its salient landmarks lay in darkness or were farther away than they ought to be. Family history flickered inside his head jerkily and uncertainly, like images projected there by an amateur and incompetent cinematographer. Then, quite suddenly, memories came fluently and at an accelerating pace, rather after the fashion in which this is supposed to happen within the consciousness of a drowning man. Not that he was going to drown. It was Charles who—posthumously, as it were—was presently going to do that. He himself was going to tread dry land again; was infallibly going to do so, even although the wheel against which he was now leaning had, several days ago, abruptly ceased to have a rudder at its command. Everything of that kind would sort itself out. He had no problems he couldn't confidently handle—not until that landfall came and he was among his own kind again. It was then would come the tug-of-war.

The direction Arthur Povey's thoughts now took was such as to make him pause at one point and ask himself whether he was in at all a normal state of mind. If he were not protected by the solitude of ocean might he possibly be saying and doing things which would constrain people to come and lock him up? Might he not, at least, be taking some first and irretrievable step in a rash and insufficiently considered direction? His present situation—although he firmly repeated to himself that it fell a long way short of the desperate—was not of a kind a man would willingly confront himself with. Still, it did seem likely to afford ample opportunity for reflection.

And now he noticed that his dead brother was still not quite reduced to anonymity. Round Charles's neck there hung a fine silver chain carrying what, in time of war, had been called an identity-disk. In certain services it had been worn on the wrist, and been so constructed that, like a handcuff, it wouldn't come off. That had been so that they couldn't too swiftly *make* you anonymous. Nowadays, people who went adventuring (and poor old Charles had been convinced he did precisely that) frequently provided themselves with such a possession—envisaging situations in which it might be beyond their power to name themselves, to remember their blood-group, to announce their having this or that physiological idiosyncrasy which meant that one or another rashly injected drug would kill them. Charles had even obliged Arthur too to wear one of these things—much as some men thus secretly wear a cross, an image of St Christopher, even a piece of sheer cabbalistic nonsense.

Indulgently, almost absently, Arthur Povey removed the

chain and its graven legends from Charles Povey's neck.
Charles was going to need nothing of that sort now—so let
him go out of the world precisely as he had entered it. And
not even ineffectively and impermanently swathed in
canvas. The vast powers of working nature, embodied in
that unslumbering oceanic swell, would contemptuously rip
away anything of the sort swiftly enough. Let Charles
descend stark into the deep, and the currents set about the
trivial task of picking his bones to whispers.

The moment, in fact, had come. Arthur gripped Charles
by the ankles. He did this—and then he looked about him,
scanning the surface of the void waters guiltily, as if to make
certain of being unobserved. The heave, the shove, required
unexpected and surprising effort. It was only a matter of
the inert weight a dead man presents. But the effect was as
if Charles—unreasonable and recalcitrant now as always—
was reluctant to go. But go he must. And he went finally
with a very small splash. It might have been no more than a
pebble that made those rather beautiful spreading concentric
rings on the water.

Arthur Povey made his way below. He got out the first-aid
kit. There were bandages, swabs, even sutures and needles.
He boiled water. Taking the greatest care, he sterilized a
knife.

II

SIR JOHN APPLEBY glanced in the direction of the South Pole. It was really, he supposed, like that. Far below this terrace on which he sat, the city of Adelaide sparkled like a profusion of gems poured out at random from the black velvet jewel-case of the night. *Une parure de diamants,* as a dealer in such things might say. The spectacle was not quite so dramatic as Rio de Janiero viewed from a similar elevation, but it was roughly in the same class. There were the same constellations overhead—the Southern Cross, and Orion upside-down—and the same atmospheric clarity produced the same effect of the stars above and the street-lights below as positively shouting at each other.

But let your gaze pass between the two—and what was there then beyond the invisible horizon? A little to the left lay the Coorong, a two-hundred-mile strip of something or other making no great impression on a map. A little to the right was Kangaroo Island—no more than six or seven times the size of the Isle of Wight, and so even less conspicuous in terms of the scale upon which nature built in this hemisphere. Between the two stretched Encounter Bay. (The explorers of Australia, Appleby reflected, had possessed a flair for naming both places and creatures which Adam in his Garden might have envied: cheek by jowl here were Cape Catastrophe, Mount Remarkable and Dismal Swamp.) In Encounter Bay you would be unlikely to encounter much. And beyond it—an empty four thousand miles off—hovered the chilly goal attained by Roald Amundsen on December 14, 1911.

Rather vaguely—for the dinner just concluded had been

an excellent one—Appleby endeavoured to visualize the South Pole. As a small boy he had naturally thought of it as something actually sticking up out of the snow—rather in the manner of the candle from the icing of his baby sister's first birthday-cake. He knew it couldn't have been placed by men, since it had already been in position when the first men arrived. Was it perhaps something that God had failed to tidy up after finishing the Creation? Or had it—at least at the start of things—had a functional significance? That was probably it. God, having fashioned the earth, had taken its North Pole between his finger and thumb and set his vast new top spinning upon a South Pole mysteriously poised in space. It had been a humming top. That was why there was something called the music of the spheres.

Accepting brandy from his host (not Australian brandy, although the wine had been wholly admirable Australian wine), Appleby progressed to less childish, yet still relaxed, musings on his present situation. The astronomical infinitudes the silence of which scared Pascal may be appreciated by anybody who steps into his Kentish or Berkshire garden on a starry night. But the answering vastness, by any human measure, of man's own speck of dust within them has to be traversed to be realized. Even then, modern modes of locomotion can delude you. When Appleby had last flown from London to Naples he had almost missed the Alps through secluding himself for a couple of minutes in the plane's loo—whereas Hannibal must have been constrained to acknowledge such natural calls scores or hundreds of times as he scrambled across them with his elephants. Years ago, Appleby had made the trip from Cape Town to Fremantle on a freighter; and that had been quite something. On the present occasion (having succumbed to the persuasion that sea voyages are restful) he had crossed the Pacific on quite a fast liner; and that had been the real revelation. There were people who said it could be done, and had been done,

in rafts or in dug-out canoes. There were people who—
apparently quite unconcernedly—made such passages as a
one-man show. Appleby reflected soberly on the existence of
such supermen. He had never, so far as he could remember,
encountered one of them. They set sail from Vancouver,
from Lima, from Valparaiso, and eventually turned up in
Sydney Harbour (which was quite worth turning up in).
They were then accorded civic receptions, and received
telegrams of congratulation from the Queen. And quite
right, too.

'My dear Sir John, I hope it isn't too chilly for you out here?'
The eminent physician whose invitation Appleby had
accepted set down the brandy and reached for a box of
cigars. His name was Budgery, and it appeared that he was
the university's professor of clinical medicine. He wasn't
what one might crudely think of as a colonial type; he had
all the polish you pay extra for in Harley Street or Wimpole
Street. 'How fortunate,' he was now murmuring, 'that the
excellent Mr Castro still consents to export these trifling
luxuries. They are no less lethal than the Jamaican sort—
but preferable, if one happens to have the habit of them,
wouldn't you say?'

'Thank you very much.' Appleby took a cigar. 'And I
don't feel at all chilly. Although no longer, on the other
hand, decidedly the reverse.'

'It has certainly been one of our warmer days. But the
cool change has turned up. You will sleep soundly, I'm glad
to say, even down in that hotel.'

'They have air conditioning, as a matter of fact.'

'Ah, yes.' Budgery clearly thought poorly of air-conditioned
hotels. 'But the old fashioned among us still have faith in
living up here, you know. And in digging our houses well into
the side of a hill. This one—my great-grandfather built it—

has a whole storey pretty well underground. We can dwell as troglodytes all summer long, if we have a mind to.'

'A most judicious disposition of things.' Appleby looked down at the city. It was an early March night, and all through the day the plain had swum in staggering heat. Even up here in the Mount Lofty range it couldn't have been exactly temperate. 'The hall porter told me there was coming up a change.'

'His precise expression, that.' Budgery laughed comfortably. 'You have an ear for idiom, Sir John.'

'Just where does the change come up from?'

'From Antarctica, one must say.' Budgery's gaze went in the direction to which Appleby's own had lately travelled. 'You are looking down on what—on the dry-bulb thermometer—is about the hottest capital city in the world. But Mount Lofty looks to Mount Erebus and Mount Terror, and in that direction our nearest neighbours are the penguins.' Budgery appeared to take pride in these geographical and zoological circumstances. 'The region gives a puff from time to time, and Adelaide's temperature drops dramatically.' Budgery's hand went to a pocket. 'Matches, Appleby?' he asked politely, and passed on to other guests.

Two or three 'Sir Johns' and then 'Appleby'. English, not American, conventions. It seemed a rather homeward-looking part of what had been the Empire long ago. Appleby sat back and lit his cigar. Even the dinner-jacket he'd been given a hint to don. But then there had been a hint, too, of something mildly formal about this all-male dinner at Budgery's house. Presumably Budgery was a bachelor. 'A few of us who dine together from time to time,' the professor of medicine had said. It was some sort of dining-club, in fact —and when playing host one could ask a guest of one's own from outside. Appleby, doubtless naively, was impressed by meeting ordinances so familiar so far away.

Appleby conversed with Mr Justice Somebody. You

couldn't have anything more English-sounding than that. The judge knew about Appleby, and expressed civil interest in the lectures he had been giving to certain higher echelons of the Australian police. But he was also taking pleasure in revealing his own extensive acquaintance with members of the English bench and bar. He told a story about the Lord Chancellor, and drove the point home with another about the Lord Chief Justice. Appleby, himself acquainted with these legal luminaries, listened respectfully, but didn't pretend to be awed. From Adelaide you could now fly to London and back for a short week-end—to shoot a few pheasants, say, or attend the Lord Mayor's Banquet. But the brute distance remained. So there lingered this business of Home Thoughts from Abroad, and of people not knowing how lucky they were in what they still lurkingly thought of as their outposts, even their banishment. There must have been plenty of times when Roman Bath was a lot more salubrious than the city of the seven hills itself. But that wouldn't have prevented prosperous Romano-British gentry—taking the waters, pottering in the baths, enjoying the excellent provincial restaurants of Aquae Sulis—from nostalgic chat about their connections with Top People in the palaces of Rome the Great. Distance lent enchantment to the view. Appleby found himself wondering what else it did. Take crime, for instance—something which the mind of a retired policeman like himself might naturally turn to. Had what might be called authentically English crime a prestige value among Australian crooks? Could an English criminal, drifting out here, exploit in this local upper class its almost unconscious assumption that it was more intimately acquainted with things English than was in fact the case? But this was an obscure speculation. It faded from Appleby's mind as inconsequently as it had entered it.

There were six men all told—sprawled or sitting in wicker chairs in a shallow arc beneath a broad verandah. The cigar smoke, bluish in a low light from two subdued lamps, blended oddly and pleasantly with the pervasive smell of the eucalypts. A couple of these nearby showed ragged silhouettes against the luminious heaven. Appleby wondered about the phrase 'up a gum tree'. If you *were* up one, it didn't look as if it would be easy to get down again. But probably the expression wasn't of Australian origin. He was thinking of enquiring about this when he became aware that conversation was fading out among his five companions. It hadn't come abruptly to a halt; people were simply permitting themselves pauses—and glances—which somehow intimated polite expectation. Appleby tumbled to it that somebody was expected to read a paper, open a discussion —something of that sort. It couldn't, fortunately, be himself : not without any advance warning being given at all. He had, indeed, found that Australians had a certain appetite for what they called lecturettes, and did at times expect impromptu performance. But this present company was of a sort which would be more considerate. Probably it was always the host who was expected to pipe up. Yes, that would be it.

This proved to be correct. Budgery had once more made the round of his guests, solicitous about brandy as before. He now sat down, and everybody looked at him in a convention of keen expectation. Probably he was going to produce a manuscript from a modest inside pocket, and deliver himself of it after some apologetically-toned preliminary word. Appleby experienced, once more, the sense of familiar matters in hand.

There was, however, no manuscript. Budgery spoke fluently and coherently without note. Moreover, he took evident pleasure in the exercise. It was quite probable, Appleby thought a shade apprehensively, that he could keep it up indefinitely.

'We are all very glad to have Sir John Appleby with us

this evening, and only sorry that he will not be staying longer in Adelaide. He goes on to Perth tomorrow, it seems, before flying home. We all believe that there is much to be said for Adelaide—including the fact that not much is said about it in the world at large. We live in a kind of pastoral seclusion, which is a pleasant thing; indeed, it is almost Arcadian in some regards. Of course, we do keep our standards as we may. I hope Appleby has found that our policemen behave well. If he were a medical man, I don't think his visit would altogether discourage him. And we would have liked, all of us, to show him more. Instead, we have to wish him *bon voyage* almost as we welcome him. *Ave atque vale*, in fact. May he drop down at Heathrow as fresh as paint in a few days' time.'

Budgery paused, and these courtesies were decorously supported by a murmur from his companions, none of whom had set eyes on their subject before this dinner-party.

'Thank you very much,' Appleby said. 'I shall always remember this delightful evening.'

Appleby believed these words to be a polite fiction—which was certainly how they would be estimated by these punctilious and agreeably clubbable persons. The event, oddly enough, was to prove them to have possessed a certain prophetic quality.

'I must confess to being a little relieved,' Budgery went on easily, 'that I haven't, by some stiff coincidence, chosen to ramble to you this evening on some stray fragment of criminal experience. I'd be a sad amateur at that, I need hardly say. South Australia does, of course, turn up some bizarre mysteries and even atrocities from time to time. But I hear of anything of the sort very much at second hand—forensic medicine being no line of mine. It's true, indeed, that what I want briefly to recall falls within a discipline almost equally peripheral, so far as I'm concerned. The story is one upon which the voice of psychiatry could well make itself heard. So it's a pity that no psychiatrist is among our number.'

Perhaps a somewhat self-conscious proem, Appleby told himself. And one faintly gathered that, in these antipodean regions, any mad addiction to the speculations of Sigmund Freud and his successors would be regarded as an indecorously new fangled thing. But at least it was somehow possible to guess that Professor Budgery wasn't going to be entirely a bore. He possessed the art of the build-up. It was quite probable that he possessed the art of the story-teller as well. Mr Justice Somebody, an elderly and heavily-built man with habits which might conduce to drowsiness at an hour like this, was plainly going to pay attention to his host. Appleby himself could certainly do nothing less. He suspected that comment might subsequently be required of him.

'The episode I shall tell you about,' Budgery continued, 'took place several years ago. It concerns a yacht I shall call the *Jabberwock*, and a yachtsman I shall call Buzfuz.'

'A lawyer?' Mr Justice Somebody asked sharply.

'Ah, there you have me.' Budgery was delighted. 'I have chosen the sobriquet badly, my dear George. Dickens's Serjeant Buzfuz is a false association. My man was almost certainly not a barrister—and if he had embraced any other regular profession, I never heard of it. He was a man of means—almost assuredly of substantial means—but more than that never came to me. Unless one is engaged in some advertising venture, one can't in these days, I imagine, scour the oceans in a costly one-man contraption without being, as the young people say, in the lolly.' Budgery paused on this, perhaps to mark his command of an up-to-the-moment demotic vocabulary. 'But you must allow me to continue calling him Buzfuz. I have so denominated him to pupils from time to time. No names—no real names—no pack-drill, eh? One rather clings to those tricks of professional reticence.'

'Then Buzfuz let him be,' Mr Justice George Somebody said judicially. 'And now, Tim, go ahead.'

So Professor Timothy Budgery went ahead.

'I've spoken of one-man contraptions. The *Jabberwock* was that in the sense that it could perfectly well be sailed single-handed. But Colin Buzfuz—I must give him a Christian name, for a reason you will presently appreciate—commonly pottered about the globe with a companion. And that's important. There are men, you know, who crave for absolute solitude as desperately as others may crave for a woman, or an addictive drug, or just for the bottle. The early history of this continent is full of what we call loners. And our tramps—Swagmen is our word, Appleby—often qualify as being just that. However, that's by the way—and irrelevant, since the Buzfuzes were not Australian.'

'The Buzfuzes?' Appleby said.

'There were two of them, as you must presently hear. But the immediate point is Colin, who could take fair doses of solitude, but was not temperamentally one of those fanatics for it. And he had the bad luck to have rather too much of it thrust on him in the end. Not that it wasn't—or that much of it wasn't—his own fault. One has to admire him, in a way. I'm bound to admit I admired him myself, even although his foolhardiness resulted in his becoming a considerable nuisance to myself and other people. He had felt a challenge, I think one may say, and been not quite certain that he had adequately faced up to it. So he tried again. One doesn't care to speak of these things—but breeding does count. Colin Buzfuz was one of us.'

Appleby (who had certainly never expected to hear this celebrated Conradian sentiment drop from living lips) felt it incumbent upon him to nod gravely. He also wondered whether the tempo of the narrative might with advantage be speeded up.

'Was Buzfuz driven mad?' he asked.

'Oh, most decidedly—although not, fortunately, in a permanent way. And not spectacularly, either. In fact, it was some time before we tumbled to the thing. Indeed, it might have escaped us entirely—and, I suppose, with the oddest consequences—if I hadn't myself, through pure good luck, happened to get at the truth of the matter.'

'My dear Tim,' the judge said, 'none of us doubts that you will be constrained to exhibit yourself as having displayed uncommon perspicacity. But proceed.'

'Very well, George, I'll proceed.' Budgery had accepted the small barb with good humour. 'And I'll begin with the *Jabberwock*, when it came sailing up St Vincent Gulf. There was nothing out of the way about it, except that it had evidently taken a bit of a battering. More exactly, it had done that, and had then in a rough and ready way been fitted out again. This was evident when people got round to inspecting it. The steering mechanism might have been repaired by a village blacksmith; a jury-mast had been stepped but was now lashed to the deck once more; the mast actually in use might have been waving in a jungle no time ago. And so on. I'm no authority on such things.

'Well, this craft, it seems, had come up the Gulf in a perfectly commonplace and unnoticeable way, and had steered into the Outer Harbour. And there, under the nose of that week's mail-boat—a whacking great Orient liner— it simply started tizzying around. Somebody got aboard, therefore, and what they found was this chap Buzfuz in the last stages of exhaustion and inanition. He simply had to be carted off to hospital.

'I needn't tell you that it didn't make much sense. Wherever he'd come from—and his log-book was a blank for weeks—he must have made his landfall quite some time before. Had he passed through the Tasman Sea? It can be the hell of a stretch of water, they tell me, whether for vessels large or small. But after that—or even if he'd come from the South Ocean by way of the Great Australian Bight—he'd have been virtually in traffic lanes during what must have been his final desperate days. Or why hadn't he simply put into Victor Harbour in the one event, or into Port Lincoln in the other? He'd have found a passable hotel—and more than passable doctors, had he wanted them—in either of these respectable resorts! Instead of which, you see, he was determined to honour us here in Adelaide. Did he imagine that, outside its capital cities, Australia is inhabited only by blackfellows hurling boomerangs? It's an intriguing thought, but unfortunately it won't wash. Buzfuz proved eventually to be a highly educated chap.

'In fact, we were left with two possible explanations of this odd nautical performance. The man may simply have been holding tenaciously to a fixed purpose. He had set out for Adelaide, and was determined to make it. Tenacity was at least a quality we had to credit him with in a general way as soon as we began to get hold of something of his story. On the other hand—but, of course, the two explanations don't totally exclude one another—he may have been quite dotty for some time—more or less capable of navigation, but in some hallucinated state which precluded a rational course of action.'

'Perhaps Buzfuz believed himself to be still surrounded by blue water.' This suggestion came from a man called Merryweather, whom Appleby had at once recognized, upon being introduced, as the most notable person present. The name of David Merryweather was written rather large in the annals of antarctic exploration. 'But I don't know that such an error would be a hallucination,' Merryweather went on. 'A fellow is hallucinated when he believes something— or somebody—to be there that isn't there at all. It's always been my guess that the albatross in the poem fills the bill. I can't remember whose poem, but it made a tremendous

impression on me as a kid. Started me off, really.' Merryweather, who was about seven feet tall, and broad in proportion, suddenly blushed like a girl—being moved to indict
himself, it was to be supposed, of egotistical interruption.
'Sorry,' he said. 'But interests me, rather. Happened to me.
Suddenly a third fellow tugging the sledge. Useful—if he'd
really been there. Unnerving, since he certainly wasn't.'

'Perhaps,' the judge said, 'this unfortunate patient of Tim's
had an experience of that kind. Tim, what about that?
Might he have miraged up a second man, tugging at the
ropes with *him*?'

'Nothing's more probable.' Budgery nodded appreciatively.
'His brother, you know, Colin Buzfuz's brother Adam.'

'And now let me go on.' Professor Budgery had the art of
smoking a cigar as he talked, but had paused briefly to give
a critical eye to it. 'Our distressed mariner was immediately
hospitalized, and I soon heard enough about him to take
over his bed myself. For days we monitored him—my two
housemen, my registrar and I—pretty well round the clock.
I tell you, I sat by the fellow myself for an hour at a time!'
Budgery chuckled. 'And the others shared out the remaining
twenty-three hours between them.'

'Capital!' Mr Justice Somebody said. 'But it wouldn't
work on the bench.'

'I suppose not. The chap in the dock would object, eh? But
now I'll tell you. Colin Buzfuz's was an astonishing case of
intermittent retroactive amnesia. He had a memory on which
the curtain went up and down much as in the theatre at the
end of a pantomime. It eggs on the audience to applaud,
doesn't it? We were almost applauding ourselves.'

'This was simply the result,' Merryweather asked, 'of his
having had a thin time?'

'It was obviously more than that. The aetiology, when we
untangled it, was fairly complex. There was the hunger and

thirst and exposure—which must have counted for a good deal. But he'd been clipped on the head when his mast came down. Or so he said. There was no physical sign of it by the time we examined him. But then a quite surprisingly long period of time was involved. Months had passed—months, I tell you!—since his first disaster had overtaken him. There's always something honestly physiological at the bottom of those capers of the mind, if you ask me. A trauma, in the only exact sense of the word. Not that his immaterial part hadn't been under stress as well. His brother Adam had been killed before his eyes—and when they were bang in the middle of the Pacific, and a thousand miles from anywhere.'

'When that mast came down?' Appleby asked.

'It seemed to have been then—and his own clip on the nut as well. He was left in a bad way, but managed to step the jury-mast, and just went on sailing. He remembered clearly—in moments when he remembered anything clearly —that he'd twice got into regular shipping routes, and actually been hailed on several occasions. There must have been craft that would have been glad enough to pick him up and turn an honest penny on him. But he sailed on like the Flying Dutchman.'

'Wasn't there a look-out for him by that time?' Merryweather asked curiously. 'All that sort of thing is very well covered nowadays, so far as the high seas go. A fellow has to make for my old haunts if he wants to remain unpestered. Even quite small craft with nothing but corpses aboard can be quite a hazard. So Flying Dutchmen aren't encouraged.'

'Perhaps not. But that sort of crazy traipsing round the seven seas pretty well on duck-boards and on 2,000 calories a day has become uncommonly fashionable. People disappear for years on end, and nobody bothers about them. Or so I gathered. And loners tend to be loners in the domestic sense as well. He travels the fastest who travels alone, and so forth. No waiting wife or weeping kids.' Budgery said this with a snap suggesting that, despite his sociable airs, he was a lonely man himself. 'But to proceed. Colin Buzfuz ended by running aground on a cannibal isle.'

'Buzfuz,' the judge said, 'seems a less and less appropriate name for the fellow. But we are all agog. Did he suffer a further traumatic experience in a cooking-pot?'

'Not so far as his recollection went. The cannibals enjoyed many of the blessings of civilization—but not, it seems, that of wireless telegraphy. There was a trading post, manned by a Dutchman of a wholly non-flying order, and a vessel put in four times a year to pick up cargo. Lord knows what. Copra, would it be? Or perhaps just coconuts.'

'Copra is coconuts, my dear Tim,' Merryweather said tolerantly. 'Do step on it. The hour grows late.'

'Very well. Colin Buzfuz put in a perfectly agreeable three months on his island, marred only by that blankness of mind from time to time. *Typee*-stuff, one supposes. Dusky beauties. And not even a dose of the pox anywhere.'

There was a faintly disapproving silence, which Budgery thought to dissipate with more brandy.

'And then?' the judge asked.

'That's the end of act one. Act two opens with Buzfuz simply having the *Jabberwock* patched up by his copper-skinned cobbers, and then off he set again. Whereupon the real horrors began. The chap had the very devil of a time. Eventually he arrived, safe but far from sound, in our extremely dismal Outer Harbour. You remember what is first to greet one? A hoarding announcing that some soap or other is guaranteed under the pure food act. The land of the sapophagi, one might say.' Budgery paused on what was evidently a favourite joke. 'But at least he was an object of considerable curiosity. Even our excellent Governor came down to the hospital to have a chat with him. Unfortunately he was in a coma at the time. Buzfuz, I mean, not the

Governor. My God, how we fought for the life of that much-travelled Odysseus!'

'Well, we pulled him through—and filled our note-books meanwhile. He really *was* of interest. You see—and here's the really weird thing—he wasn't at all sure which brother he was.'

There was another silence—decidedly an impressed silence, this time. Adelaide's professor of clinical medicine had clearly reached the denouement of his narrative. It was difficult to see that anything more could follow.

'Unique in the literature?' Appleby asked respectfully.

'Oh, absolutely. We raked through everything we could lay our hands on. No trace of such a bizarre disorder anywhere on the record. In a general way, I suppose, it was classified within the area of disassociation of the personality. But none of the mad doctors—and the world is full of them nowadays, God knows—had ever run up against this particular quirk before. Here was a man claiming—quite confidently, and as soon as he was in a state to claim anything at all—to be Adam Buzfuz, the younger of two brothers who had set out from England on a crack-pot voyage in the *Jabberwock* donkeys' ages ago. The yacht was his brother's property, he explained, and his brother's name was Colin. He had been simply crewing for Colin, as he'd done once or twice before. He rather suggested, at the same time, that he knew a good deal more about the sea that Colin did.

'Not unnaturally, we started off by accepting all this as gospel. It tallied with the ship's papers, and with the log-book Colin Buzfuz had kept almost to the moment of that mast's coming down in a storm and killing him. After that, there was every appearance of Adam's having taken over the keeping of a proper record—only very imperfectly, as one might expect from his recurrent amnesiac condition. In fact, it occurred to nobody to doubt that it was a fellow called

31

Adam Buzfuz whom, with such skill as we possessed, we were nursing back to life. It was quite a shock to me, I must confess, when I discovered we were wrong. More significantly, I had to consider what sort of shock it was going to be to *him*, when we explained to him that he wasn't the chap he supposed he was. There seemed to be a case for going about the job gently.'

'Very judicious,' Appleby said. 'But just how *did* you discover the truth of the matter?'

'We had a pretty bad slip-up, for a start. Our patient was tricked out with an identity-disk, which is decidedly a device for identifying people. But one of my young men, having no notion we were going to have a problem on our hands, simply noted the patient's blood-group, stowed the thing away, and forgot about it. It came back into his head in the end, of course, but not before we'd suffered quite unnecessary bewilderment. He got a bit of a rocket, as you may well imagine.'

'It was Colin's identity-disk?' Appleby asked.

'Certainly it was. But let me get the sequence of events right. Here had been Adam Buzfuz, as we supposed him to be, tucked up in my intensive care ward, and doing not too badly. It struck me, however, that we ought to get hold of his medical record, if it could be done with any reasonable speed. And—sure enough—in a file on board the *Jabberwock* were the medical cards of both the Buzfuz brothers. That means no more, you know, than a British National Health Service document, with a number to it, and the name of the owner's G.P. But it enabled me to cable home, and Adam Buzfuz's history came out to me in a matter of hours. It recorded nothing of the slightest interest. But it did *fail* to record something! My patient's left hand was minus its index-finger—the consequence, clearly, of an accident, and not a congenital malformation. But there was no mention of anything of the sort on the record.'

'Nor—I'd suppose—need there have been. Or not positively.' The judge said this. 'Various obvious explanations are possible. So I don't, my dear Tim, really see—'

'Quite so, George, quite so.' Professor Budgery was delighted. 'And that makes all the odder what I was suddenly prompted to do. It was something not altogether regular, perhaps. *Colin* Buzfuz was no patient of mine. A dead man can't be anybody's patient, can he? So cabling to *Colin's* doctor for *Colin's* record was not quite the thing. Still, I did it. And what did I learn? That Colin Buzfuz had lost his left index-finger in some domestic accident or other as a young man. It was when I was still chewing over this that my young fool of a houseman remembered the identity-disk. So that was that. Here, snug in bed, we had a character called Colin Buzfuz pretending to be his own younger brother Adam.'

'Pretending?' Merryweather asked.

'The wrong word, of course. *Convinced* he was his own younger brother Adam. Better still just taking the thing for granted. He was Adam; he'd seen his elder brother killed, and he'd consigned him to the deep; and now here he himself was—after the cannibal isle and all the rest of it.'

'He was now giving you a whole story?' Appleby asked. 'Talking reasonably and coherently, except just for this single curious misapprehension?'

'Just that.'

'Do you know,' a voice said out of the darkness of the verandah, 'I don't find this at all strange? People do at least forget their own identity from time to time—just as we all forget other people's, or at least their names. For instance, there was Dr Tennyson—the poet's father. He went to call on a new parishioner, and the servant who opened the door asked him his name. Dr Tennyson couldn't remember his name, so he turned away and took a walk through the village to think the thing out. He met a rustic character who tugged his forelock and said "Good day to 'ee, Dr Tennyson"—or words to that effect. "My God, my man, you're right!" Dr Tennyson said. And so he was able to get on with the day's work. Amnesia is simply a grand name for commonplace occurrences of that sort.'

'Very good, William!' Budgery said cheerfully. 'A capital story. But you must admit that my patient went one stage further. He believed himself to be somebody else.'

'Nothing to that, either.' William, who sounded younger than his fellow diners, was airily dismissive. 'There's a kid in Freud who was convinced he was a cock. He'd do nothing but crow.'

'Identification even with inanimate objects is not unknown.' Appleby was prompted to join in this amiable fun at the expense of Adelaide's professor of clinical medicine. 'My own grandfather actually died while believing he was a motor-car. Not that he was simply at the wheel of one, but that he *was* one. His last breath went into making what he judged to be the appropriate noises. Of course, cars weren't so thick on the ground then as now.'

'Which is a relevant point, no doubt.' Budgery was entirely amenable to nonsense. 'You might have expected my patient—who, unlike Appleby's grandfather, survived— to suppose himself a yacht. Not a bit of it. He was simply his own brother. A remarkable instance—don't you think? —of family solidarity. But there was a real problem. Don't shut me up before I come to that. What the devil was I to do?'

'Nothing at all, I'd suppose.' It was the young man called William who said this. 'If Colin *wanted* to be Adam, why not let him be—at least for the time being? It wasn't doing any harm. Unless, of course, you were beginning to get enquiries from relations, and so on.'

'There wasn't a chirp of that sort. And, as a matter of fact, leave the thing alone was pretty well what I did. You

34

see, the delusion didn't remain a settled one. Quite suddenly the chap would be talking about his poor dead brother Adam, and would accept without protest or any appearance of bewilderment remarks implying that he himself was Colin. That, it seems, is how dissociated personalities work : first one takes over, and then the other. I read it all up, and thought the situation out for myself. I wasn't at all keen, if the truth be told, to let my patient fall into the hands of the professional alienists. They'd simply start telling him he was in love with his mother, or God knows what. Drive him a damned sight madder than he was already.' Professor Budgery delivered himself of this persuasion with complete assurance. 'After all, the chap was sick, but he was on the mend. He was putting on weight, and there's really nothing more definitive than that. And a better circulation of blood to the brain : in proportion as that happened, all this confused thinking about himself would fade out. Time was on his side—and on mine.'

'Did you discover,' Appleby asked, 'whether they occasionally knew about one another's existence?'

'What's that? Oh, I see! It can be expressed—can't it? —schematically. A person suffering from this sort of dissociation sometimes believes himself to be A, and sometimes B. A may know of the existence and erruptive behaviour of B, and B of the existence and erruptive behaviour of A. Alternatively, A may have the advantage—so to speak— over B, or B may have it over A. The one may know he possesses a dual personality, and the other may not. Yes, my dear Appleby, I've read all about that too. Most interesting, I agree. But I confess to being a practical man. My job was simply to coax Colin into asserting himself; into keeping his chin above water, so to speak, for progressively longer periods each time he surfaced. It required a good deal of tact, I'm bound to say. Colin could be encouraged, but Adam didn't at all care for being contradicted or snubbed. Colin came in time to discuss his aberrations rationally, but when it was Adam who was around he went on—you might say—fighting for his life.'

'It's rather curious,' Merryweather said, 'this spectacle of an older brother *wanting*, so to speak, to be his own younger brother. I'd be less surprised by its happening the other way on. Did you gather that the dead man, Adam Buzfuz, had had about him anything that was particularly enviable? Would he have been more successful, or wealthier, or in the enjoyment of better health, or a more attractive personality than Colin? If I had to guess, I'd put my money on Adam Buzfuz's having been a more popular boy than his elder brother. A thing as batty as this you've been telling us about is said to have its roots in childhood, more often than not.'

'It has its roots, if you ask me, in a casually encountered virus, or—as in this case—in a blip on the head.' Budgery was robustly sceptical. 'And, in Buzfuz's case, it all cleared up. As soon as we got him ambulatory, the bouts of amnesia, or fugue, or whatever it was to be called, contracted sharply. Within a month, he was himself again. The expression is rather apt, wouldn't you say?'

The company seemed to agree that it was apt. Appleby was conscious of a faint stir, as if people were beginning to think of dispersal and bed.

'And did Colin Buzfuz depart as he came?' he asked. 'Simply board the *Jabberwock* and sail away?'

'Not quite that. He told me frankly that if he sailed in her again, his memories of poor Adam's end might be too much for him. So he simply sold her for what she'd fetch. When we discharged him he spent a couple of weeks convalescing at Government House. The Governor—who, as I've mentioned, was interested in him from the first, took rather a fancy to him. When he did leave Adelaide it wasn't to go direct to England, but to look up some distant relations in New Zealand. I believe he stayed with the Governor-General there—no doubt with a letter of introduction from our own worthy representative of the Crown. Colin Buzfuz was very presentable, you know—very presentable, indeed. I did a certain amount of fixing things up for him myself. Small legal matters arising from his brother's death, and so forth. Generally ironed things out.'

'A very odd affair, my dear Tim. We're grateful to you for entertaining us with it.' The judge said this as he got to his feet. 'What's the fellow doing now?'

'Colin Buzfuz—as I've persevered in calling him? I haven't the slightest idea.'

'You never heard from him again?'

'Never.' As he gave this reply, Professor Budgery seemed rather struck by it.

'Not even a Christmas card from somewhere? Or a crate of whisky or champagne?'

'Definitely not. A little ungracious, perhaps—but, of course, the whole episode had been uncomfortable and even a shade humiliating. He just forgot about us, I suppose.'

'Pathologically, perhaps?' This suggestion came from Appleby—who was also on his feet—on a casual and tentative note. 'I mean, his illness may have recurred in a severe form, and he may remember nothing about Adelaide whatever. I'd hate that to happen to me. It has been a most delightful evening.'

And Appleby and the judge drove down to the city together. Despite the cool change, it was a progressively warmer air that blew gently through the car.

'Curious yarn,' the judge said. 'Curious thing to choose to tell us about. Did you have that feeling, at all?'

'Yes, I think I did.'

'Incomplete, somehow. A final turn or twist or *éclaircissement* missing. Tim Budgery's a very old friend of mine.

37

Self-confident type, as you must have noticed. Doesn't like to feel he hasn't got the full hang of anything. Do you know what I thought? That this blessed Buzfuz affair still puzzles him. So it nags at him, and that was why he was prompted to come out with it.'

'I haven't your sense of his character. But I'd judge something of the sort not improbable.'

'One gets chronically suspicious, of course—sitting all day on the bench. But do you know what, at one point, came into my head? That there was some monkey-business behind the whole affair.'

'I'm in agreement with you there, too.'

'Listen! What if—' The judge checked himself. He was plainly sleepy. 'No, no, my dear fellow,' he said. 'No affair of ours. Let sleeping monkeys lie.'

PART ONE

Vacillations of Arthur Povey

III

I<small>T</small> <small>WAS IN</small> the nature of the case that when Arthur
Povey decided to assume the identity of his deceased elder
brother Charles he had very little notion of what he was
letting himself in for. He was relying, in the first instance,
on something he was shrewd enough to realize as being
unlikely in itself to take him very far : the fact of a strong
physical resemblance between the dead man and himself.
They were not, of course, twins, but their constitutional
near-identity was of the sort that 'identical' twins alone are
much on record as exhibiting. This extended to tricks of
posture and, more significantly, to the finer inflexions of
speech. In their boyhood their father, although he was an
amateur musician and therefore presumably possessed of a
good ear, had been unable to distinguish between their voices
coming to him over the telephone or even from the next
room.

But a man's identity—his *quidditas*, as the learned might
say—consists largely in what has happened to him in both
a recent and a distant past; in this and in the multiplicity
of his relationships with adjacent persons and things. These
facts make successful impersonation very difficult indeed.
Arthur Povey, estimating his chances, had to admit to himself that he faced, moreover, exceptionally formidable
problems here. Since growing to manhood, he and Charles
had been by no means intimates—or had been so only
intermittently and under the special circumstances of their
nautical expeditions. At times on the high seas Charles had
talked about himself and his affairs a great deal. But the
exercises had been plainly in the interest of relieving his own

tedium rather than of entertaining his brother; he had seldom troubled to elucidate anything not immediately comprehensible; and as a consequence Arthur had frequently paid very little attention to what was being said. Just how much he did know about Charles's life as a result of these confidences he found it not easy to estimate. What had chiefly made a mark on him was any expatiation upon those of Charles's circumstances and opportunities which it was impossible not to envy him. Charles was wealthy, and many of his recitals had this basic fact as their background. When cuisine on board the *Gay Phoenix* grew monotonous Charles would recall elaborate meals in the great restaurants of Europe. When very justly bored by the stupid erotic novels he would talk in alluring detail about his women.

There were times when this got Arthur hopping mad. If Charles was a bit of an amateur at sea, he was certainly nothing of the sort in bed. But—just as with the restaurants —his expertness was unashamedly built on money. Although the women he had slept with, or even briefly kept, were surprisingly numerous, they were also, it appeared, almost without exception celebrities. Celebrities, that is to say, in their own line. For the civilized world—so far as Arthur Povey could make it out—was likely to harbour at any one time a hundred or so courtesans of absolutely top quality, learned in their mystery to what the poet calls the red heart's core. They lived, perhaps, rather a monotonous life—somewhat like that of top tennis-players circulating from tournament to tournament. Still, they made a good thing out of it. When you took it into your head to want one you had to be prepared to pay up.

These Paphians, like the restaurants, had their *spécialités*, and in these Charles appeared to have acquired a connoisseurship, or at least a knowingness, just as he had in the world of race-horses and sports-cars and executive jets. Arthur Povey was quite sure he didn't want an executive jet. He was less certain about most of the abundant other things that money could buy.

Charles, if expansive on the theme of purchasable pleasures, had become of recent years somewhat reticent upon the subject of money itself. Arthur had no idea of what his brother was worth, and he felt (very mistakenly, as it was to turn out) that the degree, or even order, of Charles's wealth didn't greatly signify. It was by many times greater than anything he was ever likely to command himself. The point of the matter lay there.

But there was another important fact about Charles as a man of property. It hadn't rooted him in any way. Without surviving parents, or wife, or siblings other than Arthur himself, he rendered an effect of keeping all his associations on an impermanent and casual-seeming level. All those mistresses he boasted of, for example. They appeared to have been acquired, without exception, on a hire-and-fire basis. A score of times—Charles had brutally said—was as often as any rational man could want to have any individual woman. And, after that, the last thing you proposed was ever to see her again. Business affairs, of course, had to be different. A high degree of continuity in their direction was presumably a *sine qua non* of successful tycoonship. But, even here, Arthur had derived a strong impression that Charles was remote and elusive; that he had adopted the role of a mystery figure behind the scenes such as it isn't too difficult to create in a world of sprawling and gargantuan enterprises. There was a kind of modern folk-lore or mythology that made such behaviour possible. Of course the new Charles Povey must continue to employ a small nucleus of henchmen and servants in some sort of regular contact with him. Beyond that, was there any reason why he should be more than an occasional signature at the foot of a document? And the signature presented no difficulty at all. Arthur had enjoyed several weeks' leisure on the bosom of the Pacific for the perfecting of it.

Behind the signature—Arthur had begun by reckoning—it should be possible, with luck and cunning, to live for quite some time—or at least for long enough to convert into highly negotiable form some sizeable fraction of Charles's fortune. Shortly before leaving England with his brother on the last and fateful voyage of the *Gay Phoenix* Arthur had come upon an article about Charles Povey in the 'business and finance' section of a weekly paper. There had been a lot in it about Charles's activities which Arthur hadn't much understood or bothered about. But there had also been a certain amount of stuff written from the personal angle which was much more interesting. Charles wasn't exactly a recluse or an eccentric, but there was at least a suggestion that he was veering that way. It was clearly a *persona* that had, paradoxically, the seed of popularity about it. Aristocratic eccentrics—of whom the English have always been inordinately fond—are nowadays in short supply. Millionaire eccentrics are an agreeable second best. If Charles Povey, having been at least intermittently elusive for a long time, took a sudden steep dive into greater seclusion, nobody would be particularly surprised, let alone offended. Moreover, Charles was self-evidently so revolting a character (his brother piously reflected) that a great many people would be enormously relieved if he was no longer seen around.

Calculations of this sort had been much in Arthur's mind when he made his great decision. If he could have believed that he would be in any degree his brother's heir—and, as Charles's only living relative, he had surely been entitled to such an expectation—his plan would never, of course, have entered his head. If he had even felt there was any possibility of receiving a paltry legacy of twenty or thirty thousand pounds, he would probably have held his hand. But Charles had made it perfectly clear that nothing of the sort was going to happen. He had actually once declared—absurdly, and when in his cups—that he wouldn't be a bit surprised if, after his death, it proved that there wasn't a bloody penny for anybody—not even so much as would endow a cat-and-dog home. He had also said, more soberly if even less amiably, that money would demonstrably not be good for Arthur, and that he wasn't going to burden himself with the grave responsibility of letting him have any. Sometimes, and when thinking over these exchanges, Arthur found himself wholly surprised that his brother had suffered mere death by misadventure. It seemed unbelievable that he hadn't himself despatched Charles with a marline-spike.

Luck and cunning. He had enjoyed the first and exercised the second—he frequently told himself—in the highest degree among those idiotic Australians. Professor Budgery's character and persuasions (particularly his distaste for qualified alienists) had been an enormous piece of luck which he himself had exploited (he modestly reflected) with something like genius. For could anything short of genius, he asked himself, have hit upon that brilliant technique of double bluff? Not that 'double bluff' was anything like an adequate term for characterizing a stratagem of such absolute felicitousness as had come to him. Determined to steal the shoes of his elder brother Charles, he had contrived the effect of having those shoes forced, as it were, on his reluctant feet. Budgery and his assistants had been manoeuvred into believing he was the brother he was not, and that only in his own disordered imagination was he the brother he was. They had taken a great deal of credit for handing him back what they thought to be his true identity when in fact they had been furthering him in usurping a false one. It had been exceedingly funny, but it had been exceedingly useful as well. Had he turned up in Australia simply claiming to be the wealthy Charles Povey, and with a story of having buried his younger brother Arthur at sea, he might almost at once have found himself confronting immigration officials or lawyers or bankers prompted to inconveniently stringent demands for proofs of his identity. As it was, that batch of doctors had—all-unconsciously—generated a kind of vested interest in there being no doubt about the matter. And through Budgery, and when convalescent, he had been wafted into circles too exalted to admit of any suspicion blowing about at all. He was not merely the wealthy and probably influential Charles Povey; he was in some small degree a public hero—as well as enjoying, in a more restricted circle, the interest attaching to a most unusual medical history. He had been surrounded, in fact, by a benevolent regard, and everybody had taken him for granted throughout the subsequent protracted period of foreign wanderings during which he had cautiously felt his way into his new identity.

All this was very satisfactory to remember. It was, in fact, so satisfactory that Arthur Povey sometimes experienced a certain annoyance at not being able to remember it more clearly. Since those first dreadful moments in which he had stood staring down at his dead brother on the deck of the *Gay Phoenix*, the course of his life had been crowded, eventful, and often extremely alarming. It had also been a triumphant success, and in the light of all this it didn't surprise him, let alone disconcert him, that his memory commanded much of it in vivid and almost hallucinatory detail. There was something patchy about the effect, all the same. For example, he didn't really remember with any certainty how he had come to think up the turn he had so successfully put on in the Adelaide hospital. It must have started up in his mind like a creation, he supposed. But the moment of its inception eluded his recollection. So did much in the stages of its development. But then he had been in a pretty bad way—physically, of course—by the time he brought the *Gay*

Phoenix to port. No doubt he had a little piled it on—his exhaustion and all that. But he had been through experiences —totally unplanned experiences—which hadn't been funny in the least. So his memory was a trifle shaky as a result.

'Bless me, if it isn't Master Arthur!'

These words—which were all too plainly potentially disastrous in themselves—were the more alarming because of something quite unaccountable in the circumstances of their delivery. Arthur Povey, although now, as it were, fairly well established at the wicket, was still subject at least to an intermittent feeling that he must continue very carefully to play himself in. At these times an inconveniently strong sense of nervous strain might result, and to cope with this he had developed what proved to be a tolerably sufficient, and certainly very simple, resource. Just as batsmen at the crease are rather oddly permitted to do, he would declare himself unwell and retire for an interval to the pavilion. In Povey's case, when he was in England, the pavilion would be some vast and expensive (although gastronomically primitive) seaside hotel. England is a free country; you don't have to carry papers and identify yourself wherever you go; you simply choose any name you fancy, don a pair of large dark glasses, stuff some convenient receptacle with ten-pound notes, and find yourself as free as the wind. The wind, of course, is sometimes displeasingly chilly even in Eastbourne or Torquay. But unless you happen to be experiencing at the time a period of such extreme celebrity or notoriety that the press is after you hot-foot, you are as safe as houses for as long as you please. And the sort of people who frequent such hotels, although necessarily in the enjoyment of a substantial prosperity, were remote in their social contacts from those circles which Arthur as Charles was beginning at other times confidently to frequent.

So here he was—sitting in sunshine on a broad terrace,

with his monstrous hostelry behind him, and nothing except a small table, a balustrade, and the English Channel in front. Yet these shocking words had been more or less breathed in his ear. *Bless me, if it isn't Master Arthur!*

He turned his head, and found himself at gaze with Butter. His memory was at least good enough to recall Butter at once. He did so even although he certainly hadn't set eyes on the man for a very long time indeed. Butter had been a junior and somewhat anomalous manservant in the ancestral Povey home, hovering between house and garden according to the varying needs of the establishment. It didn't look as if Butter had much flourished since. Although now so plainly middle-aged, he occupied—Povey saw at a glance—a lowly station in the hierarchy of this hotel. He wasn't even a fully accredited waiter. He was one of the unassuming characters who go around emptying ash-trays, and whom nobody thinks to tip. This was surprising in itself. Povey had a distinct recollection of Butter as rather an astute and quick-witted young man, who had more than once proved uncommonly useful in getting him out of a scrape. Probably he had taken to drink. Members of the lower classes who were a little too clever for their station but could find no way out of it often sought to resolve their sense of frustration that way.

The present moment, however, was plainly inappropriate for general reflections of this sort. Here was a crisis—not of a wholly unprecedented kind. Arthur Povey, accustomed to living dangerously, took it in his stride.

'No, no,' he said, easily and pleasantly. 'My name isn't Arthur. You've mistaken me for somebody else. And rather impulsively, I'd say, since you could see nothing but the back of my head.'

'But that's just it, Master Arthur!' Unexpectedly, yet with an odd effect of the rolling back of the years, this depressed menial person flashed at his former employer's younger son a momentary wicked grin. 'It's the way the hair grows on the crown of your head. Up and forward-like—and I remembered it at once. I could always tell you from Mr Charles at a glance, that way on. Very rare it is—hair growing that way. At least among the gentry. Almost a plebeian note, it might be called.'

'My good man, you are talking nonsense.' This time, Arthur Povey spoke with a justified frigidity. 'I advise you to go about your business. Do so, and think no more of the matter. I should be most reluctant to lodge a complaint.'

'I'm sure you won't do that, sir. It wasn't your style, anything of that sort.' Butter showed no sign of budging. 'And quite thick we were, in an earlier time.'

There was a moment's silence. Povey, who had a martini in front of him, allowed himself an unhurried sip. But his mind wasn't equally leisured, since the situation was developing in a manner that made rapid thinking necessary. It was perfectly true about his hair. The point, although extremely trivial, was one he ought to have attended to. What ought he to do now? The discreet thing would be to have one more shot at simply shaking Butter off.

'I've no doubt you've made an honest mistake,' he said, with a return to a benevolent manner. 'Quite an amusing mistake, really. All that about hair, and so on.' He finished his drink, and then pointed to the empty glass. 'Just ask them to bring me another of those, will you?' He put his hand in a pocket. 'And here's for your trouble.'

Butter picked up the glass obediently, and accepted the coin. But he stayed put, with that wicked grin on his face again.

'The name's Butter,' he said. 'You wouldn't recall it, sir?'

What Povey recalled was that Butter was a man of guile. At any moment he might manoeuvre his adversary into a false position. Blank denials, if they had later to be retracted, might prove very awkward indeed.

'Butter?' Povey repeated. 'Not so common as Butterfield

49

or Butterworth. But I may well have come across the name.'

'And your own name, sir. It wouldn't be Povey?'

This had been a masterly pounce. Blankly to deny one's true name on challenge seemed a more drastic deception than simply registering in a hotel under a false one. Or so, whether logically or not, it seemed to Arthur Povey now. The result was a moment's hesitation; and this, in turn, had the effect of somehow giving the game away. He saw that he must fall back on what might be called his second line of defence.

'Yes, it is,' he said briskly. 'I'm here incognito, if you know what that means. But my name is certainly Povey. And your own, for that matter, does now come back to me. You had a job at Brockholes as a lad, hadn't you? And we did get on together quite well. Only you've got your Povey boys sadly muddled, I must say. Perhaps it's not surprising after all those years.' As he said this, Povey put both his hands on the little table in front of him and drummed on it gently. 'I'm Charles Povey, not Arthur.'

'*Charles* Povey?' Butter repeated the name slowly. It was as if he had been taken aback and was playing for time.

'Your employer's elder son, not his younger one. I suppose you remember *that*? My brother Arthur is dead, Butter. He lost his life at sea.'

'I remember Master Charles, all right. And I've heard a bit about him since. Became uncommonly wealthy, they say.'

'Not all that wealthy, Butter. But certainly I'm quite prosperous as business people go.' Povey managed an unconstrained smile. 'At least I can run to this sort of hotel—and a decent tip to an old acquaintance.'

There was a moment's silence. Povey's smile had brought back Butter's wicked grin. Or perhaps the reference to a tip had done that; its hint of more cash possibly passing had been a confession of weakness and a mistake. Butter was discernibly baffled, all the same. His gaze had passed from

Povey face to Povey's hands; had passed to his mutilated left hand.

Povey allowed a couple of seconds for the penny to drop.

'Ah!' he said. 'I can see you've remembered something. And about the right man this time, I hope.'

'Master Charles's hand was like that. Happened when he was quite a grown lad, it did.'

'It did, indeed. And that clears things up, I think.'

'It must have taken nerve, that must.'

'What's that?' It had been less Butter's words that startled Povey than the sudden respect of the tone in which they had been uttered.

'But nerve you always had, Master Arthur. It looks as if it won't do to lose it now.'

'Butter, you are talking complete rubbish—and offensive rubbish at that. I am prepared to treat it as that, and let the matter drop if you go away at once. But I warn you that a magistrate might take a much more serious view of your behaviour. It could look very like an attempt to extort money under threat.'

'Come, now, Povey—who has talked about money? Nobody but yourself with your bloody tip. And it's a fair cop, you know. That hair, that finger, Charles Povey being up to the neck in the lolly, and somebody's brother lost at sea. It adds up only one way.'

'And just what does it add up to? Arthur Povey had turned very pale. He was angry, but he also had to acknowledge to himself that he was thoroughly frightened as well. The feeling came to him chiefly as a sense of isolation and loneliness. Those first moments on board the *Gay Phoenix* when he had realized his brother was dead and that his only companion was the ocean came back to him vividly as he braced himself to look challengingly at Butter now.

'Partnership, Povey.'

'Partnership! What the devil do you mean?'

'Your partner, I am. That's what the sum adds up to. And not your sleeping partner, mind you. I'm not that sort— prepared to sit back and collect regular. A bit dull, straight blackmail, if you ask me. I wouldn't care for it. Scope— that's what I need. I've always known it. Just give me scope, I used to say. But nobody listened. "He's a damn sight too clever," they'd say. "I don't trust him." Silly of them. Even when they weren't fools themselves. I wouldn't call you a fool, you know. But there were times when your wits were the better for having mine added to them. Like when you stole your brother's money-box and couldn't think who to put the blame on. I got you clear of that one, didn't I? Coming events, Povey. Coming events casting their shadows before.'

These remarks considerably impressed Arthur Povey. His recollection of the unfortunate affair of Charles's money-box was not particularly vivid, perhaps because his boyhood had been fairly prolific in episodes involving the irregular transfer of private property. But he did remember, on that occasion as on others, calling Butter to his aid. And if Butter had been clever then, this interview was affording striking testimony that he wasn't other than clever now. His reasoning had been as sharp as his observation. Within ten minutes of spotting that small idiosyncrasy on the crown of the head of a hotel-guest casually remarked, he had cracked Arthur Povey's secret and possessed himself alike of the basic facts and of the motive of his imposture. The missing index-finger hadn't stumbled him for a moment. He had simply opined (what was perfectly true) that it had taken nerve to mutilate oneself in that way.

Arthur Povey had got thus far in weighing up these un-expected and alarming facts when it occurred to him that his conversation with Butter had already become injudiciously prolonged. In a hotel of this kind a guest is no doubt privi-leged to chat affably to a passing servant for as long as he chooses, regardless of the extent to which he is thus keeping that servant from his proper occasions. But in the present colloquy any close observer might already have sensed something a little odd. Indeed, a solitary man a little way down the terrace, although ostensibly dividing his attention between a drink and a newspaper, seemed to Povey to have been sending a searching glance in his direction from time to time. Povey had become very sensitive to anything of this sort. Since his brother's death, he had achieved what he had set out to do. But as that achievement would be judged highly nefarious if brought within the knowledge of the law, it followed that for Povey, in a strictly literal sense, the price of liberty was eternal vigilance. It was a condition from which he was coming increasingly to feel that it would be agreeable to take occasional time off.

'I think,' Povey said, 'we had better continue this discussion elsewhere.'

'Fair enough.' Butter picked up an ash-tray from the table, tipped its contents into a bucket he carried, and restored it after a perfunctory rub. 'But don't fancy you can cut and run, mate. Not so that it will do you any good. I have my resources, I have. Be up with you in no time.'

'I have no intention of cutting and running. And I'll meet you as soon as you finish work.' Povey had regained a measure of confidence. 'Anywhere you like.'

'Much obliged, I'm sure, sir. And spoken like a perfect gentleman, if the expression may be allowed me.' Butter accompanied this ironic obsequiousness with his most malicious grin. 'Cock and Bottle, then, at nine sharp. Opposite the bandstand, it is. So facing the music you'll be, in a manner of speaking, Mr Charles I-don't-think Povey.'

IV

ARTHUR POVEY WENT in to dinner in a mood of
some discouragement. The head waiter was solicitous in his
attentions and suggestions, since he had somehow divined
this guest's outstanding financial rating. Povey, however,
found he wanted to eat very little. The wine waiter had to
hover at his side for a full five minutes—a circumstance
extremely irritating to other and thirstier diners—while he
scanned the establishment's entire vinous resources with his
attention really wandering elsewhere. He then ordered a
bottle of the most expensive claret on the list. This was an
unsophisticated act, which lowered him considerably in the
wine waiter's estimation. It was also injudicious, since the
further conference with Butter that lay ahead of him
eminently called for a clear head. A waiter of inferior consequence wheeled up a trolley of elaborately bedizened scraps,
orts and broken meats. Povey eyed these starters with gloom,
and plumped for the simplicity of a small pallid chilly fish
masquerading as a trout. The waiter evinced a disposition to
throw in some mushed-up cauliflower and a spoonful of olives
which appeared to aspire to the condition of dried peas.
Povey rejected these otiose delights so sharply that several
people looked round at him. Then he began his gloomy meal.

He found, oddly enough, that what at present chiefly
rankled with him was the disrespectful character of Butter's
parting words half an hour before. If this horrible man was
indeed to become his partner—he told himself—he would at
least insist that he keep a civil tongue in his head. But was
he really going to put up with Butter? That was the
question.

The simple course with Butter was to make away with him. There was a great deal to be said for this, and Povey considered the possibilities with no strong sensation of novelty. He had quite often evolved vague plans for murdering somebody (particularly his brother Charles), and if he had never got round to the actual deed this was perhaps because of a distracting plurality of candidates at any one time. As in certain sorts of reprehensible reverie, one victim tended to melt into another as the day-dream wandered about. But the present actual situation was quite different from any he had ever been implicated in before. Butter stood in a unique relationship to him, unshared by anybody else in the world. Into the mind of no other living soul whatever had there come so much as a suspicion that Arthur Povey was alive and Charles Povey dead.

Side by side with this perception there must be placed another all-important fact. The annals of fraud no doubt contain the names of imposters and pretenders whose identity had been challenged in one way or another and who had yet successfully maintained their impersonation. Given a little more luck, the celebrated Tichborne Claimant himself might have emerged triumphant from one of the longest trials in English legal history. The vast majority of such hopefuls, however, are virtually done for the moment any responsible person urges a serious doubt about them. Povey was quite clear that he was in this category. Hard as he had worked on the subject, he knew far too little about far too much of Charles's life to stand the faintest chance with a judge and jury.

It was true that Butter was a person of very slender consideration. Indeed, it wouldn't at all surprise Povey to learn that the man had a criminal record. Supposing Butter did try to expose the imposture, he wouldn't at first find it easy to gain a hearing. But he was quite cunning enough to take this into account, and to frame his plans accordingly. He would set the press on the scent. He would probably even make money out of the thing, and be revelling on the strength of it amid flesh-pots and harlots while Povey himself was languishing in gaol.

This was an intolerable picture, which swung Povey strongly in the direction of ingeniously contrived homicide. And at once a further thought sprang up. If to be done at all, 'twere well it were done quickly. Povey told himself this with rather more cogency, indeed, than Macbeth did. King Duncan had been, as it were, without beans to spill, whereas it was in Butter's power to upset a whole sizable apple-cart at any moment. More than this; Butter might at any moment communicate the information which was at present uniquely his, if not to the police, then to some low crony or confederate of his own. Butter would, in fact, be prudent to do something of the sort pretty quickly—or at least to make some arrangement for the future extreme discomfort of Arthur Povey should anything unfortunate happen to Butter himself. It would not escape a man of Butter's acuteness that he, Povey, was by now harbouring lethal intentions towards him.

Was it already, perhaps, too late? Povey asked himself this question judicially as he watched the wine waiter replenish his glass with Lafite. Could Butter by now be in a position truthfully to assert that, should ill befall him, the wicked and impudent imposture of Arthur Povey would at once, through some agency impossible to identify or circumvent, be revealed to the yet unknowing world?

On the whole, this seemed improbable. Butter's calamitous discovery was scarcely an hour old; scarcely a further hour would pass before the renewed encounter at the Cock and Bottle. The interval was surely insufficient for Butter to decide with any deliberation upon his best means of ensuring his own safety; moreover the secret upon which he had stumbled was potentially so valuable that he would be unlikely to share it with anybody in any haste; he would be more likely to think in terms of depositing in safe keeping of some sort a sealed letter to be opened in the event of his disappearance or death. Whether veraciously or not, he would almost certainly intimate the existence of such an arrangement to Povey in the near future. But nothing of the kind could have happened yet, and it would be implausible in Butter to assert that it had. Moreover Butter could scarcely apprehend the slightest danger to attend the forthcoming business meeting in a respectable public house.

Could matters be so contrived, however, that this confidence on Butter's part would turn out to have been misplaced? Was there some neat and safe way of ensuring that the undertakers would be running their tape-measure over an obscure hotel employee before the night was out?

This large question was still with Povey as he drank his third glass. He had some quite wild and desperate thoughts. If in the wretched pub opposite the bandstand he contrived the appearance of a drunken quarrel with Butter and bashed his skull in with a pint pot he would probably get off with a stiff sentence for manslaughter. But would it be any less stiff than what came one's way for forgery, embezzlement and whatever other crimes and misdemeanours were incidental, in the eyes of the law, to the perfectly rational expedient of taking on the identity of a wealthy elder brother?

Povey tried again. Could he suggest to Butter that a desirable privacy for their discussion could be obtained by taking a late evening stroll along the virtually deserted pier, and then at a suitable opportunity simply topple his victim into the sea? Unfortunately Butter wasn't a fool, and if he agreed to such an expedition—which was unlikely in itself— he would take damned good care of himself in the course of it. In fact any proposal which involved taking Butter unawares was a dead duck from the start.

Another inferior waiter had wheeled up another trolley. Povey stared in a mild nausea at the sticky or glazed or glutinous concoctions it displayed. Some looked so effectively poisonous that he would have given half his fortune to be able to ram Butter's snout hard into one or other of them. Gloomily, he waved the thing away, and called for Stilton instead. It was just after this had been scooped out for him that he became aware he was being observed.

Often enough in a large restaurant, of course, you are conscious of something of the kind. Another guest—usually a solitary one—finds himself with nothing better to do than to take a perfectly idle interest in you. He studies your feeding habits, or speculates on your bank balance or your sexual tastes. Perhaps the man a few tables away was doing no more than this. Povey was disturbed, all the same, and in a moment he realized why; here was the same person who had appeared to be taking an unnecessary and covert interest in Butter and himself earlier in the evening.

It was possible that the man's scrutiny proceeded merely from the fact that he believed himself to have recognized, behind the dark glasses, the elusive and mildly interesting Charles Povey. Although extremely wealthy (far wealthier than Arthur in his most sanguine moments had anticipated), Charles had been in no sense a prominent public figure, and identifying him would scarcely be a matter for major excitement. Still, over the past year or so he *had* been getting increasingly into the press—for the simple reason that, not being Charles but Arthur, he had been obliged rather to play up the elusiveness. It was one of the increasing difficulties of the situation that this reputation for major eccentricity was almost bound to grow. It was already turning up in the gossip columns from time to time. So here was a tolerably familiar and unalarming explanation of why this fellow was intermittently staring at him.

Povey was alarmed, nevertheless. His new and shocking

situation *vis-à-vis* the abominable Butter was quite enough to account for this; it was a state of affairs that would render anybody jumpy. But some other and obscure factor was at work, and presently it came to him. That afternoon, and while all-unconscious of what impended over him, Arthur Povey had been feeling not only carefree but positively gay, and he had signalized a state of mind not now very familiar to him by entering a flower-shop, buying a rose, and causing the young person who sold it to him to arrange it in his buttonhole. It was a pale lemon-yellow rose, perfect in shape, and the young person had named it as a Sir Henry Segrave. Sir Henry Segraves, she added, were rather hard to come by at the moment.

But now the man at the other table was wearing a Sir Henry Segrave too.

There was surely something positively paranoiac in seeing a threat in this. Povey was suddenly less perturbed about that evening's awkward turn in his affairs than about the general mental condition which his hazardously maintained deception was building up in him. The bleak fact had to be faced that a law of diminishing returns was beginning to operate. More and more anxiety, less and less pleasingly malicious glee. From the start the glee—the keen satisfaction in being so cunning that he could fool the entire world—had really been more potent with him than the gratifications inherent in his new command of everything that a great deal of money could buy. And now he was tiring; that was the truth of the matter. He needed more in the way of periodic let-up than his present plans and policies allowed for. He would have to rethink his total situation—as soon as the present crisis was surmounted. That was the lesson of this edginess about a man who happened to be wearing a buttonhole identical with his own.

But now the man—he was a florid heavily-built man—

had caught his eye. A moment later, the man's gaze shifted to his own right hand, which he raised lightly clenched and nails-upward in front of him; he then employed his other hand to polish the nails lightly with his table-napkin. It was a trivial and unobtrusive act, no doubt slightly lacking in elegance. It was also an unusual one. Povey found that he could interpret it in only one way. He had received a signal.

This intuitive conviction was perhaps remarkable in itself, but even more remarkable was Povey's response to it. Was it his instinct as a mariner telling him he must not neglect to reply? Or did he act as he did because native to him was a certain adventuresomeness, even rashness, prompting him to hazardous courses? Certainly this last propensity had been a factor in the bizarre plan he had formed on board the *Gay Phoenix*. What happened now, however, had a disinterested quality alien to that former occasion. Nothing was to be gained by taking notice of the other proprietor of a choice Sir Henry Segrave. Nevertheless Povey picked up his table-napkin, and briefly polished the finger-nails of his right hand. It *was* inelegant; indeed, he had an uncomfortable sense of it as positively uncouth. But at least it produced a spectacular result. The man rose from his table, strolled over to Povey's, and sat down. Povey didn't find this a welcome development. But whatever its purport, it would at least take his mind off Butter. He found himself producing a casual nod and smile. The two men might have been guests who had struck up just sufficient acquaintance to warrant this informal post-prandial get-together. Povey decided to play up to this conception.

'Shall we have coffee?' he asked. 'And would you care for a glass of brandy?'

'I don't mind if I do.' Although thus acquiescing in Povey's proposal, the florid man appeared a shade surprised. It was as if Povey didn't quite rate in his regard as entitled to take the initiative involved. If this guess was accurate—

Arthur Povey saw—then it couldn't very well be the wealthy Charles Povey whom this stranger was believing himself to have joined. What was happening, in fact, was not the penetrating of what might be called his outer disguise. Encouraged by this, and obeying the same sort of freakish impulse which had landed him with the fellow at all, Povey made a further hospitable offer.

'And may I,' he asked, 'send for the cigars? The Bolivar Coronas aren't at all bad.'

'Well, why not?' This time, the florid man laughed throatily. 'Good impression on anybody keeping an eye on us, eh? Goes with your role as a leisured gent well in the lolly. Not that any trailing *is* going on, I'd say. What do you think?'

'Oh, probably not.' Povey was finding this odder and odder. Just what false position that injudicious exchange of signals was getting him into he couldn't at all tell. But it was something to get out of quickly, for he had quite enough on his plate as it was. He was about to say boldly 'But I'm afraid you've made some mistake', when the florid man spoke again.

'You weren't expected until tomorrow,' he said. 'But I see you've wasted no time, and that's all to the good. We're up against a dangerous man.'

'Ah,' Povey said. It was the only noise that occurred to him.

'And a treacherous one, eh? That's what we have to know. Says he has merely left us, of course. But he's not to be trusted an inch. A sign of a cough from him, and he's as good as on the slab. Those are the orders, as you know very well. So have you anything to report in the double-crossing line? If you have—then, by God, it's curtains for Butter.'

It was a moment before the apocalyptic character of these words registered with Povey. When they did so he felt a little giddy. Indeed, it might almost be said, in the common phrase, that his head swam. His nameless companion, although now sipping his brandy with a colourable appearance of civil amenity, had spoken in a tone of quite unnerving ferocity. It was impossible to believe that he had expressed himself in terms even of facetious exaggeration. He had meant precisely what he said. And the only possible inference was that here sat an atrocious criminal, confederate with other atrocious criminals, and intent upon the destruction of Butter, a former associate, were Butter to be indicted of the slightest disposition to treachery. And through some extraordinary stupidity (such as the most hardened and cunning criminals are said sporadically to evince) this shocking scoundrel (who was now lighting his free cigar without even removing its paper band) had taken it into his head that Povey was in on the act.

The hideous danger inherent in all this was patent to Povey at once. For might not the police at any moment swoop down on such villainy, Povey himself fall into their net, and a situation result in which he could clear himself of suspicion and resolve absurd misapprehension only by submitting to the most searching inquisition? And there wasn't, perhaps, alive in England at that moment a single man who could less afford to find himself in such a position!

His first impulse was simply to jump up and bolt—literally fleeing, as it were, this risk of guilt by association. He controlled himself, however, and in a further moment the fuller, the positively weird, strangeness of his position came home to him. This gang—or whatever it was to be called—was itself on the brink of forming against Butter just that sort of lethal design which he himself—the detected and unmasked Arthur Povey—had been perpending! And it was against an unsuspecting, and therefore utterly vulnerable, Butter. Povey was certain of this. As far as those ex-associates and fellow-villains were concerned, Butter, for reasons best known to himself, believed himself to be entirely in the clear. No hunted man would have addressed himself so blithely to a new quarry (Arthur Povey, to wit) had he the slightest sensation of that hot breath on his own neck. It was only Povey that Butter would be on his guard against.

The possibilities were so enormous that Povey felt it almost necessary to spread his arms wide to grasp them to the full. And time —something like lightning speed—constituted the essence of his opportunity. This disgusting thug's absurd blunder in taking him for a member of the pack couldn't survive long undetected. He had been mistaken for somebody who was to turn up, to join in the sinister operation, on the following day. So a tremendous *tour de force* was required. Just contrive that, and these timely emanations from an underworld would do his job for him.

'Then I'm afraid that curtains for Butter it is.'

Povey found that he had produced these words without the slightest idea of how he was to follow them up. Yet his only difficulty in uttering them had been occasioned merely by a fastidious dislike of low language. They were a deliberate challenge to his own powers of improvisation and invention. And with them he had burnt his boats. It had become instantly impossible for him to withdraw from his exposed situation with some vague words about a mistaken identity. But what on earth was he to say next?

Fortunately his ferocious companion seemed for the moment to expect nothing further in the way of verbal communication. He sat back on his chair so violently that it creaked ominously beneath the strain, and then slapped his thigh with such vigour that several people glanced at him disapprovingly from the surrounding tables. His facial expression, too, had become alarming, since it had contorted itself into lines expressive of naked sadistic anticipation. It was plain that he was delighted by what he had heard, and that he very distinctly had it in for Butter, regardless of Butter's present degree of proven unreliability. Povey—who had never associated with any species of criminal, barring a few discreet swindlers in the upper and middle reaches of society—had to confess to himself that he was almost as scared of this potential ally as he was of his acknowledged adversary, the too well-informed Butter. If he didn't now play his cards well (and swiftly) he might find himself between the devil and the deep sea.

'It's that bloody big reward,' the ferocious man said with disgust. 'There ought to be a law against such things. Banks, insurance companies : they'd buy your own brother off you without a blush. Shameful, it is. Playing on human frailty. And downright bribery, with good public money passing on the quiet. You wouldn't believe.' The ferocious man was now speaking on a note of quiet bitterness. 'Creating snouts the length and breadth of the land. Snouts under your bleeding bed. Or between the sheets with you. Your own mother may be a bloody grass.'

'It's a shocking thing,' Povey said. This seemed a perfectly safe and acceptable comment, even if it was a little on the mild side.

'Just that. Creates distrust, you might say. It's that offer of £10,000 he's after?'

'It's the £10,000. He named the sum.' Povey considered this mendacious statement. 'Foolhardy of him,' he added.

'You're telling me. Bloody nit-witted thing to come out with.'

'Yes, wasn't it? But it's vanity, you know. That's the downfall of all those small fry. Vanity. Can't resist making a big mouth about something.'

'That's it.' The ferocious man nodded sagely. But then a glance of what might almost have been called dim suspicion appeared on his face. 'Say!' he said. 'How you get this out of Butter?'

'Oh, I got into talk with him. Earlier this evening, it was.'

'So you did.' The ferocious man was impressed. 'I saw you at it. Quick work. So what?'

'I got him on to his work here. A pretty low-class job. Pay's dirt, he said. He shifts dirt and he earns dirt. But he's had enough, he says. There's money waiting for him when he cares to ask for it. And for no more than a bit of information he happens to carry round in his head.'

'Gor! Did he name the bank?'

'No, no. It was all no more than hints and mutterings. But I put two and two together. That was what I'm here for.'

'True enough.' The ferocious man nodded approvingly. 'And you think he might decide to cough up fairly soon?'

'Tomorrow.'

'*Tomorrow!*' The ferocious man turned pale, and at the same time stiffened in his chair. 'He told you *that*?'

'Tomorrow as ever is,' he said, 'he's going to I knew who.'

'The fuzz?'

'I knew who. Those were his words.' Povey paused on this pedantic precision. 'I suppose we know what to make of them.'

'You're telling me.' The ferocious man—who now didn't look at all ferocious—gulped down the remainder of his brandy and dropped his half-smoked cigar into an ash-tray. He was in a panic—which was just as well for Povey's crazy deception. This particular member of the gang (Povey felt) was almost unbelievably thick. There must be others who would be more capable of assessing the situation cooly—or who would merely and simply know that Povey wasn't the man he was masquerading as. But now nobody must be given an opportunity to reflect. Imparting a sustained momentum to the affair was the single essential thing. And the thick man's behaviour was promising. He had jumped to his feet.

'Get on the blower,' he said in an agitated mutter. 'Get instructions. That's what I've to do. No time to lose, and no mistake. Found drowned in the morning—that's what Butter will have to be, if you ask me. Or a brick fallen on him. Or collided with a bus. Or tumbled downstairs after words passing with a tart.'

'Well, then—get along, man, and stop jabbering.'

'Yes, that's right.' The ferocious man had become humble and bewildered. 'Thanks, mate. I'll go.'

'And mention, by the way, that I have another date with Butter in inside half an hour.'

'What's that?' The incompetent criminal whom a benign Providence had tossed in Povey's way had taken his first hurried steps from the restaurant. But now he halted, turned round, and stared. 'You're seeing him again?'

'Yes, for a drink at the Cock and Bottle. You must know the Cock and Bottle; it's that pub opposite the pier. Listen!' Povey seemed to have been struck by a sudden idea. 'A nice lonely place by now, that pier will be. So just suggest to them that found drowned's the thing. Get you a good mark with the bosses, old boy.'

'Butter could be got out there?' The ferocious man was open-mouthed.

'Leave that to me.' Povey glanced at his watch. 'An hour from now, he'll have taken a toddle to the end of it.'

'The end of *him*, that will be, if you can work it.' The ferocious man was enormously impressed. 'But are you sure, mate? Can't afford a boss-shot, can we? Put the bastard on his guard and he'll be with the bloody fuzz before anybody can take another swipe at him.'

'Leave it to me, I say.' Povey was impatient. 'I've been there before, haven't I?'

'On that pier? How that help you?'

'On this kind of job, you idiot. These assignments are my line, aren't they? Frig off to that blower, for Christ's sake.'

66

Arthur Povey, although scarcely to be described as a man of unimpaired moral sensibility, enunciated these coarse and blasphemous words not without effort.

He was chuckling to himself, however, before this imbecile thug had vanished from the restaurant. He felt that he was more than half-way home.

V

H E W A S L E S S sure of himself by the time he reached the Cock and Bottle. It was a most respectable looking little pub, which somehow made the whole crazy project seem crazier still. The trap—the other end of the trap—was no doubt being baited now. But how on earth was he to bring off his part of this bizarrely improvised homicide? He had already decided that his chance of persuading Butter to take a stroll along a deserted pier with him was nil. And now he found that he hadn't an idea in his head. He simply had to play the thing off the cuff. It had perhaps been a mistake to drink almost the whole of that bottle of claret. On top of a couple of dry martinis it had been a bit much. No doubt it had helped him in his encounter with that horrible thickie, had given him just the extra punch needed to push that first vital manoeuvre through. But the trouble with alcoholically boosted cunning was that it treacherously faded, more often than not, at just the wrong moment. He suddenly remembered with increased misgiving that he had drunk a companionable brandy as well. So here was a minor problem dead in front of him: just what, if anything, it would be judicious to recharge the battery with now.

And he knew there was another problem, although he found it hard to pin down. Macbeth on the blasted heath, advised by the Weird Sister to be bloody, bold and resolute, must have felt rather as he was feeling now, must have wondered whether any of these qualities was his in a measure quite adequate to the job on hand. That was it. He couldn't quite convince himself that treacherous murder was exactly his line. In fantasy at times, yes. But he had reached middle-age without practical experience of any such definitive violence. He braced himself, and shoved open a swing door. Butter—hopefully the doomed Butter—was sitting in a secluded corner of the saloon bar, with what looked like a double whisky in front of him. Povey took a grim resolution to try a double whisky too.

'So now we can have our chat,' Butter said. 'A quiet chat, man to man. No more of that guest and menial stuff. It's confusing.'

'I quite agree.' Povey said this amiably enough. For one thing, if he was to get Butter effectively on the spot, he must begin by successfully chatting him up. But another factor was at work in his relaxed tone. At their first encounter he had regarded Butter in the nakedness of his blackmailing design as a kind of *ne plus ultra* of wickedness, and he had been further offended by the insolent manner the fellow had intermittently assumed. But since then he had suffered his encounter with that ferocious nameless thug, and in comparison with *him* Butter appeared almost civilized. Butter was also—and here again he differed markedly from that other scoundrel—as clever as they come. Povey admired cleverness. As a virtually disinherited younger brother, it had been for a long time his own sole asset. Still, all this didn't alter the basic situation. *Delenda est Butter*. Butter must be rubbed out. The prospect of Butter permanently on his back was intolerable.

'I quite agree,' Povey reiterated, returning to their retired corner with his double whisky. 'And I've no doubt, my dear chap, that we can come to an arrangement—an accommodation.'

'Now you're talking turkey.' Butter nodded approvingly. 'No need for you and me to fall out. Let there be frankness between us, I say. That brother of yours, now. I can't say I ever much cared for him. Hoity-toity, he was. I'm the cream of the cream and you're the *hoi polloi* was his line. Even when you were using your wits to get him off a licking. He didn't care for a licking, young Master Charles didn't. Not the sort to bend over with a stiff upper lip, was he? Yellow, I'd call son-and-heir Charles.'

'Definitely,' Povey said. These remarks, which had reference to certain barbaric simplicities of discipline in the ancestral Povey home, were not ungrateful to him.

'And lost at sea! Smart, that was. You tumbled him in, did you?'

Arthur Povey was startled by this frank query. For one thing, it was astutely within the target area, although in fact it had been a corpse that Povey had committed to the deep. For another thing, there was a striking dramatic irony in the suggestion. Tumbling in was what now awaited Butter himself.

'Not exactly,' Povey said. 'Just put it that I didn't mourn him. And it's my turn to ask a question now. Man to man means turn about, wouldn't you say? So tell me, Butter. You're a hardened crook, aren't you? A crook down on his luck.'

'I am that I am.'

This reply, whether Biblical or Shakespearian in its reference, was again startling. It suggested that Butter, although doubtless of a lowly and inconsiderable generation, was something of a reading man.

'And at the moment a crook on the run?' Povey suggested. 'Hiding in that hotel from other crooks.'

'No, no—nothing of that kind.' Butter's tone was entirely confident. 'I've had unfortunate connections, I'm free to own. But no trouble in that quarter now. Your partner carries no liabilities of that sort, Master Arthur. Forgotten about, and nobody gunning for him, believe me.'

'I'm delighted to hear it.' Povey offered this comment carefully without surprise or emphasis. That Butter in this

regard inhabited a fool's paradise was an important point
clarified and to be passed over lightly. 'But you haven't
exactly been lining your pocket lately? Not much on the
way of working capital in the bank?'

'Correct.'

'Well, I can see to that. I'm a reasonable man. You've
had a stroke of luck stumbling on me in this way. I acknowledge it.'

'I'm not interested, Povey. Not in what you're thinking of.
We needn't go over that ground again. I'm a man of
imagination, you see. So just remember what I said. Scope
—that's what I'm after. You could even call it a bit of fun.'

'It's not practicable.' Povey said this firmly, although he
was conscious of feeling a certain stir of admiration for
Butter. They did have common ground. Povey himself was
now living (barring his present predicament) at ease. But he
was also living dangerously, and it was something which—
always within bounds—he had a taste for. 'Our ways are
going to part, Butter. Make no mistake about that. You
clear out, see? But you can take a packet with you. That I
don't deny. Ready cash comes to me fairly easily, I don't
deny either. Name your price.'

'I'm not naming anything.'

'Come, now. You just haven't the scale of your opportunity in your head. I'm not offering you chicken feed. This
isn't a talk about a thousand quid. Nor five thousand, for
the matter of that.'

'I'd bloody well hope not.' Butter had spoken stoutly, but
it was now clearly his turn to be startled. His eyes had
narrowed, 'Would you call yourself a millionaire?'

'Certainly I would. A cool million's not all that nowadays,
you know. Fifty thousand is what I'm thinking of, and
within a couple of days you can have it in ten-pound notes.
Do you know that that much can be got into a small suitcase? A small battered unobtrusive suitcase. It's worth

thinking over. A man has plenty of scope, as you call it, with that tucked away under his bed.'

'I might come back for more,' Butter said. 'Have you thought of that one?'

'Of course I have. That's the A.B.C. of a situation like this. And I've only one point to make about it. You'd lose a friend.'

'What do you mean—lose a friend?'

'I mean make an enemy. We're getting on quite well at the moment. But I promise you that would stop.'

Butter was silent. He drained his whisky and looked thoughtful. Povey employed the interval in glancing casually out of the window he was sitting beside. It commanded the pier—the longest pier in England, he believed. It boasted no 'illuminations' at this off-season of the year, and now displayed only a thin chain of lights. But they didn't shut it up—or not for a couple of hours yet. And by this time, somewhere in its semi-darkness, his unknown confederates would be waiting.

'It's a thought,' Butter said. 'It's certainly a thought. I wouldn't say you're not a dangerous man, Master Arthur. You were a dangerous boy at times.'

'Well, it's a thought you'd better think about. Unless of course, you're still not interested.'

'I'm bloody well not going to be hurried.'

'One man's hurry is another man's dawdling.' Povey made this not very pregnant remark at random—and perhaps to conceal a sudden sense of success as within his grasp. Butter was weakening. The prudent man in him was whispering that a bird in the hand is worth two on the bush; a concrete fortune more to be gone after than a nebulous notion of what he called 'partnership' in a hazardous deception. But Povey, if he felt triumph at thus gaining further ground, felt an obscure compunction as well. This —strange as it must appear—wasn't at all because he was edging Butter towards a sudden and violent end; it was because, as a means to this goal, he was tempting and corrupting the man; using the lure of gold to seduce him from a plan which at least had a spark of imagination to it. But this was mere sentiment, and the realist in Povey himself knew that here was no time for that.

'In fact,' he said briskly, 'I insist on settling this now— or certainly before we go to bed. I don't propose to lose sleep over it. So here's a fair offer. Accept my proposition within the next half hour, and I'll throw in an extra five thousand. Enough to buy you a nice Mercedes, that is.'

'I've got to think, I tell you.'

'Look, it's still nearly an hour till closing-time. Go and take a little toddle. Walk out to the end of that pier. There'll be a bit of a breeze out there. Clear your head.'

'Are you kidding, Povey?' It was with discouraging sarcasm that Butter produced this. 'I don't think! Haven't I admited you're a dangerous man?'

'Then stay put—or take a copper with you.' Povey laughed easily. 'Not that you couldn't be quite clear that nobody was following you. The first couple of hundred yards of the thing are as bare as a baby's bottom. But forget it. Just a thought again.'

'Well, well! Do you know, I think I'll take your advice?' Butter had lounged to his feet, and was evidently amused. He seemed, in fact, to have thought of some witticism that appealed to him. 'But then you're rather given, aren't you, to shoving inconvenient persons into the briny? So you must give me your word you won't follow me and do that. Your word of honour as an English gentleman, Povey old boy.'

'I give you precisely that.' Povey successfully restrained himself from showing resentment before this impertinence. He did, however, emit a sound expressive of impatience. 'But, no—we'll damned well settle this now. Sit down.'

'Too late for giving orders, Povey. You'll be lucky if

73

you're not taking them from now on. Back in twenty minutes—and just you stay put. Nice to have that word of honour, of course. But—do you know?—I rather think I'll glance over my shoulder from time to time.'

Few mental exercises are so satisfactory as the leisured contemplation of one's own cleverness. Arthur Povey was now in a position to address himself to it. Deciding that his handling of the situation abundantly entitled him to a second whisky, he made his way over to the bar and obtained this. He returned to his seat by the window and glanced into the night. The pier stretched into darkness in front of him. He fancied he could just distinguish the vanishing figure of Butter. But vanishing whither—amid what shades? *Quae nunc abibis in loca?* Povey murmured this to himself in a sudden alcoholic gloom. (His education had been of the useless public-school order.)

He realized that he was alone in this part of the pub; even the barman had disappeared behind a partition in order to attend to customers of inferior consideration. He was as alone as he had been when the last ripples had smoothed themselves out over the body of his brother in the limitless Pacific. His gloom deepened, and became tinged with alarm. He saw that he hadn't been all that clever, after all. His thinking had stopped off one step too soon. What was going to happen next? Butter's disappearance was not going to be absolute—or not unless his fellow criminals were equipped to carry off his dead body in a van, or had a launch to hand, ready to hurry it far out to sea. And certainly no qualified medical practitioner was going to turn up and sign on a dotted line that this hotel underling had died in an expected fashion of natural causes. There would be a dead body, suspicious circumstances, and a coroner's inquest. There would be police enquiries in preparation for that; the barman would be questioned, and there would be a substantial

74

chance that he himself would be run to earth. He would have to explain the very odd circumstance that he had been drinking with this menial person immediately before his death. Quite drastic consequences might follow from that.

All this was cause for uneasiness enough. But Povey felt something further. It might be described, perhaps sentimentally, as a stirring of his better nature. Poor old Butter. He hadn't been a bad chap. Impudent, possibly, and lacking in a properly obsequious bearing towards his betters. But he had been useful in his time—as in that matter, for example, of Charles's money-box. Into Povey's recollection there now oddly flooded a number of such services rendered. They added up to the reflection that Butter was a man capable of resource and stratagem in a very high degree. They wouldn't help Butter now—not with ruthless professional assassins lurking ahead of him when he was reckoning with nothing but a possible amateur assailant coming up from behind. But, given only half a chance, Butter could be your man. And it was precisely in that character that Butter had offered himself.

Arthur Povey jumped to his feet. For he, too, was a man of action. And he realized he had made a mistake.

On neither hand, as he emerged from the Cock and Bottle, did there appear to be a soul on the esplanade. He broke into a run, shoved a coin into a turnstile, and was on the pier. Broad and bare and empty, it stretched into darkness tempered only by a feeble electric glimmer here and there. Except for a low lap of water, there wasn't a sound. As yet no cry, no splash, no shot. But there wasn't much time, if any effective intervention was to be achieved. He recalled what he could of the topography of the pier, which he had never done more than scan idly as the monstrous invention of a past age. Half-way along, there was a big bulge, which must lend it from the air something of the appearance of a boa constrictor in process of digesting a baby elephant; this was occupied by a complex of tea-rooms, cafeterias, snack-bars and similar hideous haunts of the folk. Right at the end there was a yet larger area of the same sort, housing a kind of Kubla Khan pleasure-dome known as the Amusement Palace. It contained a concert hall, and presumably sundry other amenities as well. But all these places would be locked up, and didn't enter the picture. What was important was that round both these large excrescences the pier itself narrowed to a species of cat-walk, enabling the perambulating public to make a complete circuit of the entire structure without entering any of these places of further resort.

Povey was still running, and still without a plan : a combination of impetuosity and ill-preparedness alien to his normal habit, and no doubt indicative of his present radical confusion of mind. It did occur to him, however, that he ought to be provided with a weapon. The men he had set upon Butter were certainly armed adequately for their lethal intent. Probably they proposed simply to shoot the poor chap, since even respectable criminals native to these islands were now given to a quite lavish employment of fire-arms. Povey himself had never so much as possessed a revolver, although he could handle one at need. At the moment, he didn't command so much as a walking-stick.

He came to a momentary halt as the first outcrop of pier buildings loomed dimly before him. He could round it clockwise or anti-clockwise as he chose. Probably if you went right your itinerary included a Gents, and if you went left it included a Ladies. Otherwise, it made no matter. But the mere having to choose at all brought sharply to him the knowledge that he must *think*. It was no good simply charging along; he must think himself into the minds of those people—intent on liquidating their supposedly perfidious ex-associate—and calculate just what they were likely to do.

They hadn't much scope in the way of lurking-places.

There were these two long stretches of pier as bare as the back of your fist, with nothing but benches here and there, some of them enclosed in skimpy glass shelters which wouldn't conceal a cat. They'd be no good at all for an ambush. Nor could they well wait *under* the pier, in a kind of seaweed jungle of iron girders, and from there swing themselves into action as if they were a horde of jumping and clambering Tarzans. It would be in the deeper shadow of one or other of those hulking buildings that they would crouch. And probably they would choose the larger and farther out of the two : from there any untoward sound resulting from their activities would be the more unlikely to carry to shore. Moreover they would, in the first instance, let Butter pass harmless by. They could thus ensure that he wasn't being followed, either by his own design or that of somebody else. Their moment to close on him, and despatch him by whatever method they had in their heads, would be when he had almost completed the circuit of the Amusement Palace.

But surely it ought all to have happened by this time? Butter, of course, must have been well down the pier before Povey had experienced his strange change of heart and sprung to action as a result—so even if one allowed for the extravagant distance the structure ran out into the sea, one had to suppose Butter to have reached the end of it and begun his return journey a good many minutes ago. It was possible that Butter had paused somewhere en route—even sitting down on one of those benches to weigh the pros and cons of Povey's offer. In this event his enemies might well play a waiting game; if he turned back they would then pursue him down the naked pier; but they would bide their time in hiding as long as there was a chance of his going on. These considerations came to Povey as he ran on again. He didn't find them altogether persuasive. That nothing had yet happened was, indeed, crucial to any chance of success his intervention might have. All the same, it hinted at some unknown factor having entered the situation. He couldn't think what it might be, and he felt a mounting uneasiness as he ran.

There was a single bright light—almost a beacon—at the extreme end of the pier; short of that, only widely spaced pallid pools of dim radiance showed feebly in the complete darkness; there wasn't a glimmer on the sea on either side, and even the lights of the town now seemed very far away. But even in this setting—Povey suddenly realized—his own presence need be by no means indetectable. Every time he passed beneath one of those ineffective little lamps he would be visible to a vigilant eye at least as some sort of moving object. Perhaps he was being observed now. Perhaps they even knew his identity, or knew that he wasn't the accomplice that the ferocious man had so thick-headedly taken him for. Perhaps, regarding him as an equivocal and dangerous character (such as, indeed, he precisely was) they had resolved to eliminate him and Butter in one operation. *That was why nothing had happened yet.* They were somehow quietly holding on to Butter while waiting for *him*.

But by the time Povey had grasped this possible dimension of the affair, he was confronting the Amusement Palace itself. Because of the single brilliant light beyond it, it showed only as a black blank wall in front of him : monstrous and almost shapeless, like a botched silhouette. It might have been a mountain of ebony, of jet, but he knew it to be in fact constructed out of some transparent substance, lozenge-like and many-faceted, designed to flash and glitter invitingly to idle holiday-makers on the beaches and esplanade. And one optical trick was at work now. From the last of the lights strung along the pier a single beam was refracted to a point a little to the left of Povey as he stood. What it played upon—what it very mysteriously played upon—was an axe. This axe, a large and alluringly wicked-looking axe,

78

seemed to hover unaccountably in air, breast-high. Before he could in the least explain its presence, or even be wholly confident of its materiality, Povey found he coveted this axe very much. He felt at once that it was *his* axe. It was almost as if a protecting Providence had handed it down from the sky. He stepped forward, put out a hand, and touched glass.

The axe was in a big glass case, along with other impressive objects, only uncertainly identifiable, but including a big coil of fat flattened hose. The entire set-up was for fire-fighting. Or perhaps, since it was so ostentatiously displayed in this show-case fashion, it was just for impressing the clientele of the Amusement Palace with the measures taken for their safety.

Had one to shatter a large pane of glass to get at these things? That would create a frightful din. But perhaps there was a little box containing a key which could be obtained by breaking a piece of glass no more than two or three inches square; Povey seemed to remember noticing such things in theatres. He began to fumble around, gave a tug at something, and felt the whole front of the case swing open. The fire-fighting equipment was as immediately available for use as were the life-buoys which he had noticed deployed along the esplanade, each oddly labelled *For Emergencies Only*. Well, the axe was for an emergency too. Povey grabbed it.

What use would the thing be against properly armed men? Arthur Povey simply didn't ask himself this question. The untoward events in which he had become involved were possibly bringing about in him a regression to a quite primitive state of consciousness; he was like a Fuzzy-Wuzzy warrior who, having successfully grabbed his assagai or whatever, recks not that a platoon of British Tommies are after him with a Gatling gun. He even lifted the axe above his head and brandished it. For that sort of employment it

79

turned out to be rather on the heavy side. But it would really be a terrific weapon at a pinch. He had a sudden and rather heartening vision of himself taking a swipe at an enemy's neck with it, and of a head tumbling to the ground and rolling away like a turnip. So sanguinary an imagining as this showed that the Povey blood was up. He strode forward. He would round the first corner of the Amusement Palace, come upon poor old Butter ringed by adversaries and with his back to the wall, and himself sail in as irresistably as Samson when having a go at some Philistines.

This fantasy didn't realize itself. Round the corner he boldly went, to find nothing but blankness and silence. But that was how ambushes started, no doubt. With a sudden return to caution, he moved close to the big building he was now rounding, and crept forward in its deeper shadow. Then he did hear something, or thought he did. The impression was of voices far inside the Amusement Palace itself, and as he paused to listen he even fancied he saw a moving or flickering light similarly deep within the grotesque glassy structure. Then everything was quite blank again. He walked on.

He walked on and round the next corner—which was the crucial one. He was at the tip of the pier, and suddenly bathed in light from that single brilliant lamp. This was where they'd pick you off; where they'd already, perhaps, picked off Butter. He'd hardly realized his own folly before a kind of resigned terror was flooding over him; it was like knowing you were facing a firing-squad in some grossly theatrical midnight execution. But still nothing happened, and he felt a reflux of confidence which was also a sense of irrational frustration. What he was involved with was turning out to be a bizarre non-event. There *was* no ambush; there was no ambush laid either for Butter or himself. The ferocious man's accomplices (who were no doubt his bosses as well) had turned down the notion that Butter was so dangerous that he must be made away with that night; or, less thick than the ferocious man, they had sensed something phoney about the whole story, and were prudently holding their hand.

So what had happened to Butter? The answer seemed clear. He had walked right round the pier undisturbed, and he and Povey had passed each other when he was half-way back. This had been possible because one of them had happened to go clockwise, and the other anti-clockwise, round the first of the large buildings perched high above the sea. Or Butter may just have happened to drop into the Gents. In any case, Butter must be back in the Cock and Bottle now, wondering what had become of Povey, and with his mind perhaps made up one way or the other in the matter of his proposal of cash on the nail.

This was annoying. Indeed, it was infuriating. Butter wasn't *meant* to have returned. The idea had been to get rid of him. And now the pestiferous and dangerous fellow was alive and kicking, after all. Arthur Povey had quite forgotten, in this moment, that he had switched to Butter's side; that he had in fact gone to rescue Butter at great personal risk. His intentions were again entirely murderous. This rapid change of feeling—it was almost like a switch from one personality to another—displays, it must be admitted, a facet of alarming weakness in the bold schemer of the *Gay Phoenix*. It makes evident an almost crying need for a steadying influence upon his conduct.

The present effect of this vulnerability was to render him equally disgusted with these pusillanimous villains and with himself. He peered at the axe; wondered how he could have thought to derive any advantage from lugging along so imbecile a weapon; and decided a little to relieve his feelings by chucking it into the sea. That would teach the local municipality, he told himself, to expose a fairly expensive object of the sort to the whim of any predatory passer-by.

So he walked to the tip of the pier (much frequented during the day by anglers under the absurd persuasion that they might there catch fish) and prepared to comport himself somewhat in the manner of the bold Sir Bedivere when finally resigned to casting Excalibur into the mere. But as he hesitated for a moment he not only heard the water wap and the waves wan; he also heard, once again, that faint suggestion of voices—and they were now distinguishably agitated or angry voices—not far away. His grip tightened on the haft. It mightn't be a bad idea to hold on to the axe just a little longer—until, say, he was in the act of stepping off this accursed pier.

He hurried back to the Amusement Palace and down its farther side. As he did so, he heard a clock chime faintly from the town, and in the same moment found the darkness around him suddenly entire. The bright light at the end of the pier, together with the feeble overhead lamps strung along its length, had been punctually switched off on the stroke of the hour. Five minutes before, Povey might have been glad of the complete obscurity thus achieved. Now, with his sense of crisis still somewhat in abeyance, he cursed aloud. He hadn't a torch. He hadn't, so far as he could remember, even a box of matches. And what had happened was like an inky deluge abruptly poured over his head.

He stood still, supposing that, once his vision had accommodated itself to this new situation, the dim forms of things would reveal themselves against the night sky and enable him to grope his way back to the esplanade. But what did happen was quite different. He heard a faint shout—this time, triumphant rather than angry—and in the same instant darkness was turned to light. Darkness was turned to drenching and overwhelming light, so that he staggered where he stood, dropped the axe, spun round, and buried his face in his arms as if to ward off a further brutal blow. It was seconds before he peeped out from this refuge—but when he did so the appalling character of what he glimpsed jerked him into a condition of vivid perception at once. He was gazing into some hideous tropical jungle, and out of this an enormous and savagely grimacing gorilla (or perhaps it was an orang-outang) seemed about to hurl itself upon him from a tree. Moreover (as if this sudden materialisation of a large ferocious anthropoid ape wasn't enough to be going on with), this creature was patently in competition for its evening meal with an even more menacing lion crouched in a thicket nearby. The lion could be seen to be licking its chops. The gorilla had begun to sway in the manner of a trapeze-artist on its bough, as if preparing for a particular exhibition of expertness at Povey's expense.

Before these sudden untoward appearances Povey (it is only candid to admit) had uttered a terrified scream (or at least squeal) before his intellect operated on them. He then reflected that between himself and whatever hazard they represented there was interposed the barrier constituted by the glassy integument of this part of the Amusement Palace. And this clarification was succeeded by another. What he was witnessing was in fact an Amusement, and these monsters were no more than out-size automata designed for the entertainment of the vulgar. He could now see that there was a lot more of the same thing : writhing serpents, trumpeting elephants, giant vampire bats, and pretty well anything else one could think of. The only mystery was why this exhibition—and indeed, so far as he could judge, the entire interior of the ridiculous building—had suddenly burst into brilliant illumination.

'That's every switch ! We've got him !'

This must have been a triumphant shout, since the words reached Povey quite clearly. They also explained what was happening. Butter had somehow escaped from his hunters into the Palace; he had been pursued; and there had been a species of hide-and-seek in the dark until somebody had found the main switches and turned on every light in the place. The result must be that Butter's chances of escape were now minimal.

At this moment in Povey's cogitations the wretched Butter appeared. He was running away. Nothing could be more rational than such a course of action. What was disconcerting was what he was running away from. It was not from the ferocious man or his confederates, none of whom were as yet in evidence. It was from a crocodile. A crocodile is, of course, pre-eminently a creature from which to escape; the well-known fact that it is accustomed to weep while gobbling one up is peculiarly unnerving in itself. Only this crocodile (which was opening and closing enormous jaws with metronomic regularity) was of human manufacture. To the comparatively disengaged regard of Arthur Povey it was evident that it moved on some sort of concealed track or railway, much as, on the stage, does that member of its species which has so fortunately swallowed a clock in *Peter Pan*. That Butter should regard this outrageous toy as for the moment the principal hazard to which he was exposed suggested that he was not altogether adequately in command of his wits. The sudden flood of light had taken him quite as unawares as it had taken Povey. He must be imagining himself to have stumbled into a very live kind of zoo. After all, the great country seats of England now much favoured that sort of thing as attracting the profitable curiosity of the populace; it was not inherently improbable that a large seaside town should emulate them.

But now the real enemy was in sight. Across what perhaps represented itself as a mango-swamp two figures could be observed advancing upon the desperate Butter. Since the terrain was difficult their progress was necessarily slow; they ought to have been equipped, it was possible to feel, with cutlasses or jungle-knives in order to hack their way through the tropical proliferations here simulated in high-quality plastics of one sort or another. The slender coco's drooping crown of plumes was at this moment impeding one of these pursuers, and the lustre of the long convolvuluses the other —a Tennysonian note which Povey was without the leisure to appreciate. He felt that something must be done, since Butter bore every appearance of being trapped. Perhaps Butter supposed in a bemused fashion that ahead of him lay some free egress to the outer world, since from within, and in the particular conditions now obtaining, he must be looking out into darkness through whatever transparent stuff it was that these walls were made of.

It was, indeed, hard to believe that any solid barrier stood between Povey and the scene he contemplated. The labouring jaws of the crocodile seemed now to be within inches of him, so that he started back in senseless alarm; the creature, however, slewed rapidly to one side, turned on a pivot, and returned as it had come, swingeing the scaly horror of its tail. Not so Butter; he had come to a hopeless stand, realizing—or recalling, as it must be—the true facts of his case. He was like a goldfish which has formed the foolish project of moving indefinitely on a straight line, only to be confronted by the unyielding concavity of its bowl. This impression was enhanced for Povey by the circumstance that Butter's mouth was gaping open. Perhaps he was screaming to be let out.

Let out he had to be—and it suddenly came to Povey like a revelation that he had the very means of this enfranchisement in his hands. He grabbed the axe again, swung it in air, and brought it down with all the strength he possessed on the translucent surface before him. The stuff wasn't, of course, glass; it didn't behave as glass, which was perhaps just as well; but it did shiver and give, and two or three further blows punched a big hole in it. Butter, with whom the penny had at last dropped, clawed frantically at the jagged edges with his hands—but not, surprisingly, to the effect of cutting himself to bits. He was excusably in a hurry. It was true that his immediate pursuers were still labouring amid wild nature. But the total area of this particular diversion was, after all, comparatively small, and when Butter finally scrambled through the hole he wasn't much more than the length of a room ahead.

'Run!' Butter yelled, and they both ran. There was no room for manoeuvre: nothing but the catwalk between the long side of the Amusement Palace on the one hand and the edge of the pier and the sea on the other. And they were still bathed in remorseless light. It was just as Povey realized this disagreeable fact that he heard first a shouted order and then a shot. So that was it. They were sitting targets, and they weren't going to be let escape. It wasn't only curtains for Butter. It was curtains for Povey as well.

'Give me that axe!'

Butter had shouted this without checking his pace. Povey had no notion that the beastly axe was still in his possession. It was certainly of no avail against bullets, and he might as well have chucked it away at once. But now Butter had grabbed it, and swerved aside. For a moment Povey supposed he was going to stand his ground brandishing it, fall gallantly under a hail of fire—that sort of thing. But what Butter was dashing at was the side of the Amusement Palace itself. Povey had a glimpse of a box-like structure, and of what seemed a thick dark cable running up to it from somewhere beneath the level of the pier. Then Butter swung the axe, and what followed was like a gigantic flash of lightning at one's elbow or under one's nose. There was a very nasty smell of singeing, but Povey was less aware of this than of the instant return of blackest night. He supposed that he had been blinded, and then he felt what must be Butter's hand on his arm.

'Always well insulated, a fireman's axe,' Butter was saying. 'A damned close thing, all the same. Not an eye-lash left.'

'Good God, man! Did you put the bloody thing through the power supply?'

'Just that. So universal darkness buries all.' Butter allowed only a second to this exhibition of Butter the reading man, and Povey felt himself being propelled to what he knew must be the edge of the pier. There Butter paused a moment. 'Thanks a lot, mate,' he said. 'Gawd! Won't you and I go places now?' His grip on Povey's arm momentarily tightened. 'Can you swim?' he asked.

'Of course I can swim.'

'Then jump. Like this.'

And Butter jumped and Povey followed. It was a symbolic moment. They were in deep water, and had a long way to go.

PART TWO

Idle Curiosity of Sir John
and Lady Appleby

'W HENEVER I AM aware of a red-letter day,' Dr
Dunton said, 'I celebrate it by coming to tea with Lady
Appleby.' Dr Dunton paused to accept a hunk of cherry
cake. 'A red-letter day in the history of the parish, that is to
say.'

'It's a very good habit,' Judith Appleby commented, and
reached for her visitor's cup.

'But, of course, you mustn't confine yourself to them,'
Appleby said. He had long ago got quite used to backing up
his wife's polite remarks, particularly to the clergy.
'Parochial red-letter days can't, in the nature of the thing,
happen all that often.'

'Not in the popular acceptation of the term. In the strict
sense, they tumble on top of one another. Consider Trinity
Sunday. That's St Alban. And the Tuesday is St Barnabas,
and the Thursday is Corpus Christi. In between these two,
for that matter, comes the Translation of Edward, King of
the West Saxons.'

'Who translated him?' Judith asked innocently.

'I imagine that the answer must be the Holy Ghost, Lady
Appleby.' The Vicar of Long Dream had the cultivated
clergyman's fondness for decorous professional frivolity.
'Originally the term was applicable only to removal from
earth to heaven without death, as in the case of the translation of Enoch. At a later date it came to be used figuratively
simply to describe the death of the righteous. It is curious,
by the way, that the Romans spoke of a notable day as
white. Marked as by a white pebble. *Candidissimo calculo
notare diem* is an expression in Catullus, if I remember

rightly. But Sir John may correct me. Bentley in rather a notable sermon speaks of a candid and joyful day.'

'Most interesting,' Appleby said without irony. Dunton was a conscientious and resolute caller upon every cottage in his parish, and must have to manage a good deal of conversation upon restricted themes; he was entitled occasionally to expatiate among the educated. 'But just what red-letter day is this?'

'I have a new parishioner. The man who has bought Brockholes has moved in.'

'So I suppose the badgers themselves have had to move out, poor things.' Judith produced this suitable etymological joke neatly. 'The place has been deserted for ages.'

'Quite so. Savage howlings—as Pope has it—filled the sacred quires. I imagine an abbey may be called a sacred quire.'

'The place has certainly been empty and in rather a poor way for a long time,' Appleby said. 'And it will take quite a lot to keep up.'

'Yes, indeed. But already a great deal has been done. I understand there's money. A great deal of money, they say.' The Vicar gave this information casually, but it was clear he was far from displeased at the prospect of a wealthy parishioner in the person of the new owner of Brockholes.

'What's the fellow's name?' Appleby asked.

'Povey. Somebody called Charles Povey.'

'How very odd!' Judith Appleby was now genuinely interested. 'That was the name of the people there quite a long time ago.'

'Exactly. It appears that this Mr Povey has repossessed himself of his ancestral territories. Like Warren Hastings at Daylesford, the returned nabob has resumed his own. One always recalls Macaulay's splendid essay, does one not? An unfashionable writer, I believe. But I remain firmly attached to him.'

'Is Mr Povey really a nabob?' Judith asked.

'I understand him to be the modern equivalent of such a person. Tycoon is now perhaps the word. An interesting Americanism, that. The word is understood to come from the Japanese and signify a great lord.'

'I don't think the Poveys were ever great lords.'

'Dear me no, Lady Appleby. I spoke of ancestral territories facetiously, I fear. Mr Povey's father, it seems, was a man of some cultivation—or at least musically inclined. But the family is clearly not of any antiquity. Victorian industrialists, no doubt.'

'Are there to be any other members of the family around?' Appleby asked.

'I haven't heard, but rather imagine not. Mr Povey is said to have had a younger brother, who was unhappily drowned. I haven't heard anything of other relations.'

'And you haven't yet met the chap himself?'

'Not yet. In my position, you know, one must not be precipitate. Newcomers may resent the suggestion that their spiritual needs are at all urgent. Such matters, they are apt to feel, will keep. The shooting, the plumbing, the establishing themselves in the best available society : these are commonly felt to have priority. So I bide my time. If, as I greatly hope, this Mr Povey is an active churchman, he will no doubt take an early opportunity to intimate the fact. In that event, we might get things going with a little dinner-party, to which I should beg Lady Appleby and yourself to come. There would be the Bishop and the Archdeacon, naturally, since the man must be regarded as a considerable landowner. But I can promise you no positively overpowering preponderance of the cloth.'

'That would be delightful,' Judith said firmly, and Appleby remembered to produce a vigorous confirmatory nod. But then he recalled something else.

'Charles Povey!' he said. 'But of course. The name rings

a bell. One reads about him from time to time. And if what the journalists say is true, Vicar, the chances of your dinner-party mayn't be too good. He's a tycoon, sure enough, but he goes in for managing things by remote control. One hears of extreme instances of that, doesn't one? Millionaires who haven't been glimpsed for years, and so on. Rather fashionable form of plutocratic arrogance or diffidence or guilt-feeling or Lord knows what. I've an idea your chap has been drifting that way. So perhaps he has come to Brockholes to go to earth, as it were. The name of the place sounds just right for a recluse.'

'Nonsense!' Judith said briskly. A certain note of hope in her husband's voice hadn't escaped her. 'Badgers are sociable creatures. They live in communities. Perhaps this Mr Povey is going to set up a community. Brockholes is certainly large enough for it.'

'Transcendental Meditation—or something of that sort?' The Vicar, who knew that Appleby, despite much faithful reading of the lessons at matins, was as unregenerate as anybody in his parish, was quick to get in a little frivolity first. 'A rival concern just over the hill, would you say? Prayer-wheels and joss-sticks going like mad all day. However, we must welcome wholesome competition. Interesting word, *Joss*. Means a Chinese idol, and comes to us from Portugal. But it's good Latin before that—and nothing more or less than *Deus*, my dear Appleby. So one might say—from another point of view, you know—that the Blessed Rood is a joss-stick. A curious thought.'

Appleby agreed that it was a curious thought. Dr Dunton's line as a learned Peacockian clergyman, although a familiar turn during these tea-drinkings at Dream, always pleased him. He signified this by offering the Vicar another slice of cake.

'We must put this chap Povey's temperament to the test,' Appleby continued. 'He may be thoroughly genial and clubbable and convivial and all the rest of it, after all. If you feel that you can't yourself at the moment call and leave a little tract—'

'Really, John!' Lady Appleby said.

'Sir John is only quoting rather a striking poem,' Dr Dunton said comfortably. 'The shivering Chaplain robed in white, the Sheriff stern with gloom. But do you mean, my dear Appleby, that you're game to call on him yourself?'

'Why not? I ought to, come to think of it. Presumably there's no Mrs Povey, so I can't send Judith. And a stray patch of our ground—Judith's ground—runs along with his. It will be a proper civility.'

'But not while the man's still unpacking his furniture,' Judith said. She distrusted her husband when seeming to propose punctilious social courses.

'Lord, yes—if it's in a sufficiently casual way. I'll go and shoot one of his badgers—rabbits, I mean—and then drift in to apologize. Round about eleven tomorrow morning. He can't well do less than offer me a glass of Madeira. And then we'll send the aged Hoobin—our sole but respectable retainer, Dunton—over with a brace of our own pheasants.'

'We haven't any pheasants,' Judith said. 'And this, as it happens, is the month of June. St Alban, St Barnabas, and Edward King and Martyr. The sad fact is, Dr Dunton, that John has too little to do. Hoobin grows more and more tyrannical, and drives him from the garden as with a fiery sword. So he must propose to go and badger Warren Hastings.'

'Just right to badger at Brockholes,' Appleby said brilliantly, and was gratified by a responsive chuckle from his guest. 'And do you know what I'll do, Dunton? I'll say, as I leave, "By the way, we have a very good Vicar here." That's a perfectly proper remark. And it may set the ball rolling.'

Judith Appleby sighed, and replenished the teapot from the hot-water jug. She knew that here was a lost cause.

On the following day Appleby came home just before lunch. Whether he had in fact shot a rabbit was obscure. But he had to admit failing to meet Mr Charles Povey.

'They told me he'd gone to town,' he explained to Judith. 'I wasn't surprised. Brockholes is a place to escape from, just at the moment. The chap seems to have moved in there in a hurry, and there are still workmen doing everything under the sun. And furniture being unpacked, just as you said.'

'What kind of furniture?'

'What kind? Why, just the usual sort of stuff.'

'Don't be absurd, John. Nothing is more diagnostic than people's furniture. And you can describe it if you want to.'

'Perfectly true—so I can. There was a Hepplewhite tambour writing-table, and an Adam sofa with absurd sphinxes, and some knife cases pretending to be funerary urns, and rather an attractive gouty stool—'

'Being moved in? I wonder where they came from.'

'Oh, Sotheby's, I expect.'

'I don't see how you could know that.'

'Neither do I, quite. But they had an aura of the sale-room, you might say. I've a feeling that this Povey is setting himself up in a new way of life. And, of course, Brockholes has been a mere barn. It would have to be furnished again from dot. Do you think it had remained untenanted in the possession of this family of Poveys?'

'I've no idea. Did you manage to talk to anybody?'

'Of course I did.'

Judith, who had finished lunch, got up, walked to a window, and surveyed the modest garden, orchard and paddock of Long Dream Manor. Everything was in admirable order. And it wasn't really true that Hoobin declined the assistance of his employer—or of anybody else whom he could get to work for him. His nephew Solo—who must have been the son of a brother's extreme old age—had been cunningly insinuated into something like full-time employment with the Applebys, and was at this moment to be observed, as he commonly was, resting between one labour and another. It might be calculated that Hoobin and Solo did one half of the work, and that John—assisted by sundry young Applebys when they happened to turn up—did the other. It didn't prevent John from being sporadically restless in these years of his retirement. Nothing but time on his hands, clearly, had taken him pottering over to Brockholes Abbey.

'Who was it?' Judith asked.

'That I talked to? Oh, a factotum. I can't think of a better description. A fellow of the name of Bread.'

'An unassuming name.'

'He seemed aware of it. "Bread's my name but cake's my nature," he said. Quite a wag.'

'Did you feel cake *was* his nature?'

'It's an interesting question.' Appleby appeared to take this problem quite seriously. 'Nothing rich about him. But just a hint of something unexplored inside. No, more than just a hint. He described himself as Povey's secretary. I thought it odd that a secretary called Bread should make a joke about cake. And one felt he must have made it before. Rather stale cake.'

'Jokes all round,' Judith said—and felt that all this endeavour to extract interest from a man called Bread was another sign that John was still restive at having been put out to grass. Not that he had been, really. He'd asked for his cards before he need have, declaring that running the Metropolitan Police had bored him—even at £14,000 a year. And now here he was, preparing to talk nonsense about some newcomers at Brockholes. 'Was anything else odd about him?' Judith asked patiently.

'Well, you know, it's part of the job of a tycoon's secretary to get rid of people. It's his instinct, you may say. And here was an elderly gentleman patently shoving in out of the most idle curiosity. He must have felt that—just as you do.'

'So I do. But go on.'

'He chatted me up. Walked me round the place, and was extremely communicative. Incidentally, he offered me that glass of Madeira.'

'Which you politely declined.'

'So I did.' Appleby seemed surprised. 'But how did you know?'

'My dear John, all those years as a policeman have endowed you with a strong hierarchical sense. There isn't a more orthodox Establishment character in England. You must have felt that a tycoon's pucka secretary is perfectly entitled to offer you a drink. But you declined one. *Ergo*, you felt he was assuming the role without the proper credentials, however he was representing them. That he *wasn't* a secretary—or not of the sort he was claiming to be. The wrong tie. Or the wrong accent.'

'Judith, you're a perfectly horrible woman. And what you say is essentially accurate, as far as it goes. But there's a little more to it. Bread's a crook.'

'Oh, dear!'

'No, I'm *not* imagining things. Quite enough real crooks around, without having to dream them up. Bread has a beard.'

'A beard? A kind of barley bread, I suppose.' Judith made a gesture of despair. 'All sorts of people wear beards nowadays. Our own son Bobby, for instance. And Bobby's not a crook. He's a perfectly respectable rising novelist. Even novelists can be persons of perfectly impeccable life.'

'True, Judith, true. But beards, you see, always suggest to me—through long professional habit—the possibility of hastily assumed disguise. I have the trick of looking not *at* beards but *through* them. I strip bearded characters of their beards at sight. A straight habit of the imagination. Just as a dirty old man—'

'Yes, of course. So you stripped Bread of his beard. Just what charms were then revealed?'

'But seriously, Judith. I just wouldn't have *looked* at the man, *except* for his beard. But I did. And I realized I'd seen him before.'

'Well, that's a different matter, I admit.' Judith had begun to be impressed. 'Just where had you seen him before?'

'I haven't a clue. It's most annoying. At the Old Bailey, perhaps.'

'In the dock?'

'Certainly not on the bench or at the bar.'

'So where do we go from here?'

'Oh, nowhere at all.' Appleby suddenly assumed a large lack of interest in the mysterious Bread. 'If a tycoon choses to employ a shady character as his secretary it's no business of ours. Absolutely not.'

'Absolutely and definitely not.' Judith wasn't impressed. 'Bread rang some bell with you. Do you think you rang a bell with him?'

'My name might. Of course I had to give my name. That's quite possible, and might explain his doing such a lot of talking.'

'Was it just general polite chat?'

'Not in the least. It was a kind of orientation course in the character and habits of his employer. Don't you think that was odd?'

'Far from it. He wasn't seeing you as a policeman, obscurely evoking his criminal past. He was merely seeing

99

you as his boss's new neighbour, harmlessly curious as to what's cooking up at Brockholes. And he was putting you in the picture, simply in the interest of cordial future relations. But just what was the picture like?'

Appleby didn't immediately reply to this question. He was filling his pipe in the deliberate fashion he was inclined to affect when giving time to ordering his ideas. He didn't look much like a man continuing to discuss a topic of no interest to him. He had brought to a high state of development—Judith reflected—a strong natural aptitude for pouncing on puzzles and shaking them until their interlocked components fell apart. Dr Dunton had presented him with a new and shiny puzzle of this sort (not that anybody else would have *seen* it as a puzzle) and he had given it a preliminary shake or twist or twiddle that morning.

'The picture,' he said slowly, 'wasn't just of a tycoon. It was of an *embarrassed* tycoon. Financially embarrassed, I mean. Charles Povey has created—not inherited—some very large enterprises. But they're not really his cup of tea. His true mind inclines to other and higher things. So they've been inclining of late to go more than a little wrong. I was given the notion of a kind of Antonio in *The Merchant of Venice*, with his argosies going down all over the Mediterranean. The poor chap is too retiring, you see; too much given to elevated thought. Transcendental Meditation, perhaps, just as our good Vicar proposed.'

'It sounds the most awful nonsense.'

'You're right. It sounds the most awful nonsense. Or a confidential secretary's admitting and obtruding it does. But the scene was well depicted, I'm bound to admit. Quite an able character, Mr Secretary Bread. Povey, being of an extremely retiring disposition, has left matters far too much in the hands of subordinates. There's a popular view of him, Bread says, which the press has been building up, as a kind of all-powerful spider sitting in the centre of an immense web. It's a piece of minor financial mythology which I happen to know is true. But it's based on a misapprehension of Povey's beautiful character. Such was Bread's theme, copiously developed for the benefit of a total stranger paying a morning call. What do you make of it?'

'It has the air of a defensive operation.' Judith paused to consider this judgement. 'There's real trouble brewing, and entrenchments—psychological entrenchments, as it were—are being hastily dug.'

'Yes. And there was another theme. Povey has had private troubles, shocks, traumatic experiences which have borne hard upon his sensitive nature. Hence his digging in—the entrenchment image again—at Brockholes. The world forgetting, by the world forgot. We mustn't expect to see too much of him.'

'Did Bread particularize—in this business of shocks, I mean?'

'There was something about the brother—a deeply beloved younger brother—lost at sea. It was a horrible accident of some sort. Charles Povey witnessed it, and immediately on top of it came other hideous experiences. They have left him not always quite right in the head. There was a definite hint of that.'

'I'm with you that it sounds odder and odder. Did Bread give any instances of how this distressing intermittent lunacy appears?'

'He gave one instance, which doesn't sound particularly lunatic at all. Povey bolts into yet deeper retirement from time to time. Goes off for a breather under an assumed name. Perfectly innocent and reasonable, that seems to me. But Bread is worried by it.'

Appleby had joined Judith at the window, and was frowning slightly. But this expression of displeasure might have been occasioned merely by what he surveyed through the glass.

'Really,' he said, 'Solo excels himself. He doesn't do a stroke. It's the burden of his early environment, I suppose. He's been larruped around all through his boyhood. And now, because I won't let Hoobin take a strap to him, the boy conceives himself arrived in the land of the lotus-eaters. Sleep after toil does greatly please. I positively believe he is capable of sleeping on his feet.'

'Does it occur to you,' Judith asked, 'that what you've been in contact with is not so much Povey's problems as Bread's?'

'Oh, decidedly. He's beginning to organize resistance in a tight spot. Something like that. Trouble brewing, as you say. And he's building up a coherent picture designed to forestall undesirable inferences. However, it's absolutely no business of ours. I insist on that. I'm not going to be shoved into poking around in it.'

'Of course not.' Judith Appleby was just short of speechlessness before this monstrous perversion of the situation. 'Why not go out and larrup Solo? It would come as a great surprise.'

'I'm not interested in surprises. I cultivate roses. I'm not sure I don't keep bees and play the fiddle, and I'm not sure I don't feel a strong affinity with Solo. *Cum dignitate otium*. An expression in Cicero, if I remember rightly.'

'Of all the barefaced—!' Judith checked herself, since Mrs Colpoys, the Applebys' housekeeper, had appeared to clear away the luncheon. 'I'm going into Linger to shop,' she said briskly. And she left her husband to his meditations.

VII

LINGER IS A small market town disposed round a large market place. Its local paper, the *Linger Weekly*, is fond of styling it the metropolis of the vale—meaning that it draws upon the vigorous rural life of King's Yatter, Abbot's Yatter, Drool, Boxer's Bottom, Sleeps Hill, Snarl, and Long Dream itself. Persons from all these subsidiary centres do their shopping there, reaching it either in private conveyances or ramshackle and wandering buses according to their means and station. Everything parks in the market place itself, observing or ignoring a system of white lines, very up-to-date in its time and still just distinguishable on the cobbles, invented by Judith Appleby's deceased cousin, Everard Raven, barrister-at-law. The white lines radiate, like the spokes of a wheel, from a marble statue of the Queen-Empress executed by Everard's uncle, Theodore Raven, and by him generously donated to the Urban District Council upon some Jubilee occasion. One of the more obscure pubs (which are numerous) calls itself the Raven Arms.

These circumstances resulted in Judith's being accorded a certain consequence among the more historically-minded of Linger's citizens. When she went into the Linger Stores (formerly Odger's Shop) an octogenarian assistant would fish out for her a chair normally concealed beneath the counter— although in general, and conformably with the egalitarian spirit of the age, chairs for the gentry had disappeared from all the emporia of Linger with the single exception of Ulstrup the Saddler's.

Judith was thus accommodated, and going through a considerable list of requirements, when Mrs Birch-Blackie came into the shop. This represented something of a crisis for the establishment. Although Judith was Lady Appleby (and was on all occasions loudly so denominated by the well-affected) the Birch-Blackies were much grander than the Applebys. This was not at all because Colonel Birch-Blackie's father was understood to have been eminent in the history of the Sudan; it was because the Birch-Blackies, in addition to having been around for a long time, still owned more local acres than Ravens in their heyday had ever been heir to.

Mrs Birch-Blackie, however, was not one to acknowledge a small *contretemps* of this sort. She resolved the matter by sweeping from the counter sundry small tins of fish-paste and peanut butter, and perching on the surface thus cleared with all the ease to be expected of an expert horsewoman.

'My dear Judith,' she said without preliminary greeting, 'have you heard of the arrival of this absurd person at Brockholes?'

'Yes, I have. But only yesterday.'

'It has been known for some time. Ambrose has been very doubtful about it. There are rumours of some very shady connections. Although they were perfectly respectable people at one time.'

'I suppose so. But I know very little about them.'

'But you must have known the Poveys when you were a girl, surely. This man's father wasn't quite normal, of course. He went in for music and things of that sort. But they were certainly on visiting terms round about.'

'You forget, Jane, that we weren't quite normal ourselves. The Ravens, I mean.'

'Perfectly true.' Jane Birch-Blackie appeared to see no point in disagreeing with this.

'Both my uncles—Everard and Luke—never bothered much with people who didn't interest them. Of course we did meet Poveys from time to time. But my memory of them is quite vague.'

'No loss, so far as the two boys were concerned. The younger was called Arthur, and it seems he's now dead. A light-fingered lad.'

'Light-fingered?' Judith was mildly astonished. 'You mean he was known to be a thief?'

'In a petty way. Even so, it couldn't be called a nice thing in a country gentleman's son. Creates a bad impression. Not a thing one cares to see get around. Ambrose felt that very strongly when there was trouble over his cigarette-box.'

'Colonel Birch-Blackie's cigarette-box?'

'Of course it was a long time ago. When Arthur Povey was an undergraduate, in fact. And he was uncommonly clumsy over it. He let our parlourmaid see him pocket the thing.'

'That certainly wasn't too bright of Arthur.'

'The person who was bright was the parlourmaid. She might have shouted at the little brute, and there would have been a scandal there and then. But she simply went and told Ambrose. Courageous of her, really, to do anything at all. She might have been terrified and kept mum. Servants hate being involved in anything of that sort.'

'What did your husband do?'

'He was extremely upset. The box had something to do with pig-sticking.'

'How very odd.'

'I suppose Ambrose had stuck a record number, or something of that sort, and it had been given him by his subalterns to celebrate. At Poona, perhaps. If Poona's a place where they do stick pigs. Of course Ambrose tackled Arthur Povey quietly, and asked him to return the box. The young man denied all knowledge of it, so Ambrose had to tell his father. He was dreadfully in doubt as to whether it was the proper thing to do. It hadn't ever happened to him before, you see. And Ambrose doesn't like what you might call unprecedented situations.'

'What happened then?'

'Nothing at all. Arthur simply told his father that Ambrose must be potty. So what more could be done?'

'I suppose Arthur was too old for his father to larrup,' Judith said, thinking of Solo Hoobin. 'But he could have turned him out of the house.'

'I think he was resigned to Arthur's getting into that sort of trouble. It was a matter of bad associations, it seems. He had taken up with a dishonest stable-lad, or some such person. However, Arthur Povey is dead now, and we mustn't report ill of him.' As she said this, Mrs Birch-Blackie looked severely at the octogenarian assistant, who was plainly straining his decayed hearing in an endeavour to catch this notable conference between exalted persons. 'It's the elder brother Charles who has come back and bought Brockholes. And Charles was quite a different proposition. By which I mean that he showed promise of being a blackguard on a much larger scale. He burnt his grandmother's will, and when a fuss was made over that he tried to burn down the house as well. When really quite young he seduced half the girls of the village, and was believed by many to have raped the rest. And of course he successfully blackmailed the then Vicar, who was universally regarded as a man of the most saintly life. There were various other disgraceful incidents I don't remember.'

'I don't believe a word of it—or not more than every second word of it.' Judith, who had known Jane Birch-Blackie for a long time, was openly amused. 'You are simply retailing wild gossip from a misty past. If this Charles Povey was half as notorious as you suggest, he would be most unlikely to return to the scene of his misdemeanours and shamelessly set up in the old home. It doesn't make sense.'

'Effrontery, don't you think? But I didn't say he'd been exactly notorious. When you have a bad hat in the family you keep the fact as dark as may be. And being extremely conceited, he probably believes by now that he got away undetected with a good deal which in fact was known and talked about. And, of course, he has made a fortune. It appears there's no doubt about that. A rascal's fortune, one doesn't doubt. But a fortune it is. And if you're an impudent beggar already, you'll be a damned impudent beggar when on horseback.'

At this point in Mrs Birch-Blackie's discourse Judith became aware that the octogenarian, having finished making up her large order, was preparing to stagger respectfully out to her car with it. So she stood up.

'Are you going to know him?' she asked. 'Receive him, as our parents expressed it?'

'I shall let Ambrose decide.' Mrs Birch-Blackie failed to avoid the suggestion that this was a hedging reply. 'He has already made some enquiries, and it is certain that the man isn't at all well regarded in the City. On the other hand, it appears that he still belongs to a perfectly respectable club.'

'John says that you can't get turned out of a club nowadays except for pertinacious indulgence in vices simply not, my dear Jane, mentionable between gentlewomen.'

The octogenarian looked alarmed; Mrs Birch-Blackie, on the other hand, found risible the notion of gentlewomen inhibited in this way.

'I don't believe it,' she said robustly. 'From what I've heard of those tiresome places you could take your favourite pig into them and nobody would blink an eyelid. But cheating at cards, now. That must be another matter. As for this Charles Povey, I shall at least give the man a nod.'

'You mayn't have the opportunity, Jane. There's a distinct suggestion going round that he's acquired Brockholes simply to lead the life of a recluse. He'll ignore people.'

'What monstrous impertinence!' With very little logic, Mrs Birch-Blackie was extremely indignant.

'Or he may lavishly entertain his own sort of people while ignoring us locals.'

'His own sort of people? Jet-set trash, I suppose, and fashionable tarts, and unspeakably common Americans.'

'Quite possibly. And perhaps our husbands will be able to peep at the tarts while crouching lasciviously in the Brockholes ha-ha.' The octogenarian had by this time fortunately tottered out of the shop, and was thus not affronted by this ultimate frivolity between high-born ladies. 'You must both of you please come and lunch at Dream quite soon. We can have another gorgeous go at poor Mr Povey.'

'Agreed,' Mrs Birch-Blackie said briskly. 'And we'll both collect a little more information meanwhile.'

It was perhaps in the interest of this proposal that Judith made a detour by Brockholes on the way home. It was a course of action not wholly consistent with the attitude she had hinted to her husband's impulse of curiosity earlier that day. But as she now knew Mr Charles Povey to be absent in London it couldn't be averred that she was endeavouring to take a peep at *him*. And a peep at the house—she pointed out to herself—was another matter. It was a long time since she had taken a look at it. And it held an authentic architectural interest in a minor way.

Brockholes Abbey wasn't, of course, an abbey. Its stone hadn't even been quarried out of the ruins of one, since by the time it was built any such ruins there may have been had long since disappeared into dykes and hovels and pigsties. According to the learned Dr Dunton there had never been an abbey at all, but only a minor farm served by lay brethren belonging to a great Cistercian monastery eighty miles away. But since the site had at least vague ecclesiastical associations, whoever had built the existing house had judged Brockholes Abbey to be a reasonable and dignified name for it. The same general idea had led to its being designed—

although only half-heartedly—in a pseudo-mediaeval idiom.
It was really a great big square box with Gothic screens and
curtains and bits and pieces tagged on. There was a tower
which was said to afford an admirable view of the surrounding countryside.

The property ran to a small park, and it was on rising
ground commanding this that Judith brought her car to a
halt. The house, which thus stood revealed at a middle distance, exhibited nothing remarkable, except that half a dozen
cars, vans and lorries were scattered around in front of it.
What was striking was an activity going on round the peri-
meter of the whole place, and at this point near completion.
This was a wire fence of inordinate height—it must be a full
ten feet—and curving over at the top in a manner suggesting
the sort of structure designed to discourage the egress of
dangerous animals from a zoological park. Here, however,
the curve was outward-facing, as if the animals were to be
prevented not from leaving but from entering. The operation
must be costing a great deal of money—there was a small
army at work on it now—and was wildly incongruous with
the surrounding peacefully rural scene. One would conjecture
Brockholes to be in the occupancy of some section of the
investigating classes dedicated to exploring the possibilities of
chemical warfare or nuclear fission. John hadn't reported
this phenomenon; he had perhaps entered the place by the
main avenue on the other side of the house, where these
appearances were as yet not obvious.

There was only one possible conclusion: that Charles
Povey's desire for a retired way of life was mounting in the
direction of the pathological. Judith's immediate impulse was
to challenge this incipient security. John had done so, if
unwittingly, and she wasn't herself going to do less. Her resolution having been taken, she drove on, rounded the park,
and left her car near the entrance gates to the avenue. These
were open, and there was nobody around. The defences of

Brockholes—if that was the true conception of the matter—appeared to be as yet in a random state. It occurred to her that this indicated something like panic. She marched up the drive, which ran between beech trees straight to the main façade of the house. The house, thus positioned, was slightly intimidating; it rendered the effect of staring at her aggressively through a score of eyes. Of the numerous workmen who must be responsible for the cars and lorries there wasn't any sign. Perhaps they had Solo Hoobin's habit of frequent periods of repose.

She was now near enough to make out the front door. It stood within a shallow portico which left it clearly in view. Judith wondered whether it was really discreet to go farther, for it would be a shade awkward if somebody emerged from the house and accosted her. Even as she hesitated on this thought, the door did open, and what appeared to be a small group of people emerged. Then she saw that it was three people—two men and a woman—together with a couple of very large dogs. A moment later, she realized that a certain touch of obscure drama characterized the spectacle thus afforded. One of the men, who could be distinguished as holding the dogs on leads, was waving an arm angrily in an imperious gesture of dismissal or banishment. The woman, who was small and dumpy, was protesting vigorously. The second man, who was very tall, appeared to be playing a passive role. Suddenly the woman began screaming, the man began shouting, and the dogs began to bark. The effect was raucous and displeasing in the extreme, even at the remove at which Judith stood. Such scenes, she reflected, simply don't transact themselves at the front doors of well-conducted country houses. She was about to turn away, retracing her steps down the avenue, when the brawl or fracas abruptly ended. The man in charge of the dogs had stooped to them with the plain intention of letting them loose. And at this the dumpy woman turned and walked hastily away, hauling the tall man (who appeared to be of positively torpid habit) behind her.

Judith now stood her ground. Once at a safe remove from the house—the door of which had been banged to—the dumpy woman resumed her clamour. She didn't seem, however, to be shouting at her companion; her remarks gave the impression of being passionately directed at the empty air. Judith felt rather curious about them. So she waited, planted in the middle of the avenue.

'I'll have the law on him!' the woman was yelling. 'Back he comes to these parts, bold as brass, the bloody bastard! And his bleeding lordship is unable to see you, they say. And go away or we call the police, they say. And he's never heard of you, they say. Me—an honest girl that I was, doing no more than be the first to show him you know where, and that simply to oblige! I'll have him up at sessions. I'll have him before the gentry on their bench, I will. Him that's my Sammy's honest father before heaven, and never the sight of a shilling to this day. But Sammy will have his rights of the dirty bugger! Won't 'ee, Sammy?'

At this question the tall man (who might have been no more than twenty), realizing he was being addressed, oddly agitated his lower jaw, and thus produced a low effervescent sound, suggestive of the opening of a rather flat bottle of lemonade. Judith saw, with some distress and dismay, that this large person was either dumb or half-witted. Perhaps he was both. She also realized that the woman who had directed so informative a discourse to the empty heavens was known to her, at least by name, having been at one time in the employment of a near neighbour in the respectable condition of a washerwoman.

'Good afternoon, Mrs Corp,' she said. 'Is this your son Sammy?'

Mrs Corp's response to this civil greeting could scarcely have been termed rational. Mrs Corp waved her arms (actually in a theatrical rather than a threatening manner) and again addressed invisible powers above.

'And him rioting all these years with harlots in their palaces! We've heard on 'un, we have, and he need make no mistake about it. Like to fill Brockholes with them now, he be—and you the first of them, you rakes, you jakes, you painted callet!'

It was a moment before Judith understood, with a mild sense of shock, that she was now being harangued directly. This frenzied woman appeared to believe, rightly or wrongly, that the new owner of the house from which she had just been turned away indulged himself in a lavish concubinage, and that Judith herself was one of those under his protection. Although tolerably well-preserved, Sir John Appleby's wife had been for some years a grandmother, and she wasn't sure that she ought by any means to take offence at being credited with the charms of a successful courtesan. Nevertheless, it seemed desirable to get the record straight, if only to restore Mrs Corp to some more or less normal condition of mind. It had to be conjectured that she believed (or feigned to believe) that the home-coming Charles Povey was Sammy's father, and that she had visited Brockholes for the legitimate if embarrassing purpose of making father and son acquainted with one another. It didn't very clearly appear that Sammy Corp (or Sammy Povey) was a young man likely to commend himself to a putative parent in such circumstances. Nor, for that matter, did Charles Povey, by all accounts, sound a good buy as a long-lost father. In any case, the proposed *rapprochement* had not been a success. The Corps had been repulsed by some underling (perhaps John's new acquaintance Bread); and for the time being, at least, Mrs Corp was extremely upset. Whether Sammy had it in him to be upset was not, for the moment, clear.

'Come, come, Mrs Corp,' Judith said firmly. 'You ought

to be able to recognize me as Lady Appleby from Long Dream. And I have never so much as met Mr Povey, unless it was casually and more than twenty years ago.'

'And a dirty little brute he was long afore of that,' Mrs Corp interpolated with vigour. 'Wasn't there what Hannah Sloggett saw behind Scurl's barn? And what Johnnie Spawl told his ma about after Sunday School? And what Jane Grope heard her dad say he had to go to the doctor for? What about Farmer Pell's chimbley and Gammer Jemmet's nanny-goat? I ask you.'

'Mrs Corp, I know nothing about such matters.' Judith was reflecting on the alarming length of rustic memories— something which the returning Charles Povey seemed to have failed to reckon with. 'So please calm yourself. What-ever business you may have with Mr Povey, it was foolish to be in such a hurry about it. And if you feel there is something due to Sammy, you ought to have a quiet talk about it with Dr Dunton. He will give you very good advice about any steps you should take.' Judith was about to add, 'That's what he's there for,' but decided that this sense of the matter, although widespread among a harassed gentry, was not quite orthodox. 'And now,' she said instead, 'if it's of any help to you, I can drive you both home.'

'Thank you for nothing, ma'am.' Mrs Corp, it was plain, was still in a shockingly disaffected mood. 'Sammy, my poor lamb, you come with me.' And Mrs Corp grabbed her rejected son—actually reached up, indeed, and took him by the ear—and marched firmly off down the avenue.

Judith watched them go, and then took another look at Brockholes. She found she wanted to have nothing more to do with the place. She would impress upon John how right he had been in his pious reflection that the new situation there was no business of theirs. The Warren Hastings *de nos jours*, clearly, had miscalculated in any supposition that the rural populace of Daylesford would turn out with banners to welcome the restored fortunes of his house. It looked as if he was going to prove a most undesirable influence in the district at large.

And now she had better go home. But Mrs Corp, or more probably Mrs Corp's son, had upset her slightly. And the house was still glaring at her in what appeared a malign way. She found she didn't want to retreat down the avenue, with this phenomenon behind her and the possibility of again encountering the pausing Corps ahead. She decided on a small detour through the seclusion of the park.

The park was untended and untidy—and had never, indeed, been a very impressive specimen of its kind. There were a few large trees of the isolated and splendid sort, but in the main it was an affair of small clumps and spinneys. She covered this terrain briskly, and found that the house, although she was presently viewing it in flank, was still intermittently very much in evidence. Then she spotted a kestrel, a more satisfactory sight, and followed its flight. It hovered, swooped, and disappeared behind one of the spinneys. On the edge of this she remarked something else: the stump of what must have been a large tree, standing in a cleared space. Its girth was considerable, and it was about six feet high. Trees are not commonly felled at that inconvenient height, and as she walked towards it she was faintly puzzled. She was a good deal more puzzled when the stump bestirred itself and moved on.

Trees don't commonly take constitutionals—or only, she told herself, in *The Lord of the Rings*. Perhaps she was in the presence of an Ent.

It was, of course, what is called a hide. It was a hide of the portable sort, such as lovers of wild nature are solicited by their manufacturers to acquire in the interest of bird-watching. There was presumably a bird-watcher inside. Judith, although sceptical about the merits of these particular contraptions, was a bird-watcher herself, and having come up fairly close to the thing before identifying it, she now stood still so as not to disturb anything that the concealed student might be in process of observing. But now the truncated tree took another and quite bustling toddle, so positioning itself that she could distinctly see the aperture behind which a pair of field-glasses glinted. There didn't seem to be anything much to reward their scrutiny; in fact there demonstrably wasn't a bird in sight. Then an odd thing happened; from somewhere on the drive came the sound of a motor-car, and the headless Ent immediately swung round in that direction. When nothing became visible, it swung back again. Judith suddenly realized that what was under scrutiny was not the feathered songsters of the grove but Brockholes Abbey. The oddity of this prompted her, in turn, to odd and thoroughly reprehensible conduct on her own part. She picked up a stone and hurled it at the hide as hard as she possibly could.

Since Judith was a sculptress by profession, the musculature of her arms was commonly in very fair trim. Moreover, her aim was good. The impact of the stone upon the fabric of which the hide was constructed must have been considerable : quite enough to make the person tightly encased in it wonder whether he had been hit by a bullet or charged by a bull. The sides of the hide were shoved apart from within, and the flimsy structure fell to the ground. Judith found herself confronted by a justifiably angry middle-aged man.

But not by a bird-watcher. The man's mere attire confirmed Judith in this conviction, since he was dressed in rather seedy city clothes of the black jacket and pin-stripe order. One felt that the effect ought to have been crowned by a bowler hat. Alternatively, he might have been wearing a soft hat with the brim snapped down well over his eyes, together with a raincoat of which the collar was raised well above his ears. He suggested either a member of the criminal classes or a person professionally obliged to consort with such. Judith didn't take to him. She addressed him, however, in a tone of marked sympathy.

'Did the bird peck you?' she asked.

'The bird?' The man glared round him indignantly. 'I don't see any bloody bird.'

'Oh, what a pity! It was a twite. A great twite, of course. They're extremely rare in this country, and you may never have a chance to see one again. In Venezuela it's called the bomber bird. Because it dive-bombs—just as it did you.'

'I don't believe it. There's no such bird as a twite. You've made it up.' The man glared at Judith, unconscious that he had thus totally exploded his pretensions as an ornithologist. 'You've assaulted me. You might have caused me grievous bodily harm. I'll have you summonsed.'

'If you do, you'll have to explain what you were up to, skulking inside that idiotic thing in this park.'

'I was watching birds. That's lawful, that is.'

'That story wouldn't stand up for five minutes. You don't know a wren from an owl. I think you'd better explain yourself.'

'It's no business of yours. You're not the owner here—nor his agent either. So you can clear out.'

'I'm a citizen,' Judith said. 'Or is it a citizeness? Anyway, it's my duty to take notice of any breach of the law. And what you are about, my man, is clear enough. Loitering with intent to commit a felony. No experienced magistrate could have a doubt of it. You are in the grounds of Brockholes Abbey, a house into which a great deal of valuable property has just been moved. And your job is to case the joint for a break in.'

'It's nothing of the kind!' The angry man was now alarmed as well. 'You don't know what you're talking about.'

'I ought to. I'm the wife of a policeman.'

'In those clothes? You're as likely to be the wife of a rat-catcher.'

'You may even have heard of him. John Appleby.' Judith saw that this announcement had created an effect. 'And I shall drop in at the local police station and report this on my way home,' she said. 'Good afternoon.'

'Here, wait a minute!' The spurious ornithologist was fumbling in a pocket. 'I got to give you my card, I have. The firm's card. That's our instructions when risk of mis-understanding occurs in the course of our legitimate employ-ment. Here it is, Mrs Appleby—Lady Appleby, as it must be. You'll have heard of us, I hope. A highly reputable and ethical concern, I need hardly say.'

'I don't think I want your card.' Judith had glanced at it and handed it back. 'And it still doesn't explain just what you're up to.'

'Ah, Lady Appleby, that's another matter. We have very strict instructions there. Authenticate ourselves on demand—demand by a responsible person like yourself, that is. But everything beyond that is confidential. Confidentiality is our key-word, Lady Appleby. It has to be, I'm sure you will understand, in all high-class private investigation. And ours is very high-class, very high-class indeed. Crowned Heads have come to us, Lady Appleby, to say nothing of Cabinet Ministers and people of that sort. Should you ever require our services, it will be our most sincere endeavour to give every satisfaction. Satisfaction is the firm's motto, I need hardly say. So contact us at any time, Lady Appleby, without hesitation. Perhaps I might mention that matrimonial diffi-culties are our special line. Elegance, taste, economy are our watchwords for the way we go about things. Our profes-sional standards are rigid, and our results rapid and reliable.

It may truly be said of my colleagues that they come as a boon and a blessing to men.'

The unmasked private eye (as he must be called) now laughed easily—possibly to indicate that these ancient slogans were facetiously intended. But he laughed to empty air. Lady Appleby had turned and walked away.

PART THREE

Povey at Bay

VIII

A RTHUR POVEY (now Charles Povey) and Butter (now Bread) eyed one another across the dinner-table without much cordiality. They commonly dined together, and this was an index of the degree of control which Povey's secretary had come to exercise over his life and affairs. Butter— Povey had freely to acknowledge it—was a very smart chap. Although prone at times to regress upon the racy idiom of the folk, he could now put up (or so Povey judged) a very credible appearance as a minor associate of important persons. He talked a kind of modified posh which, although impure to Povey's authentic U-type ear, was perfectly adequate to his own middling station. But what was chiefly remarkable about him was his flair as a psychologist. 'You've got to take them the way they tick' was his constant advice to his employer—and he would then explain how they *did* tick. This ability was not, indeed, a wholly adequate substitute for any sort of knowledge of how Big Business is run. At least in the narrower technical sense, his ignorance here exceeded even that of Arthur Povey himself. On the other hand, Butter's former criminal career had for many years transacted itself at least within hail of robberies, frauds, forgeries and protection rackets on a very large scale, and he seemed not to find any very different climate obtaining in the world of high finance to which he had now been introduced. The City and the East End, it had to be supposed, although exhibiting to a superficial gaze markedly contrasting styles of life, were both inclined to smile upon persons who ticked after a more or less identical fashion.

An imposter who has expected to find himself in the

enjoyment of a large yet compassable competence, but who instead of this is obliged to boss, or seem to boss, a ramifying financial empire, is patently in need of the sharpest wits that he can summon to his elbow. And Butter could scarcely be faulted here. His skill in getting his principal out of tight corners—once so famously exemplified in the matter of Charles Povey's money-box—had been demonstrably on several occasions the sole means of smothering suspicions which, had they been allowed air, must infallibly have resulted in putting Arthur Povey in gaol.

Where Butter had disappointed Povey had been on what may be termed the romantic side of his nature. Butter had rejected outright the achieving of an easy affluence in the form of a suitcase stuffed with ten-pound notes. He had done so in the spirit of an active adventurer, for whom a bizarre impersonation was to be but the stepping-stone to further hazardous conquests. If he had hitherto failed here (and the whole project, after all, was nebulous), the fault had not been entirely his. Povey, a fair-minded man, was constrained to admit this. Almost from the first, he and his associate had been thrown on the defensive, and this on several fronts. It is fortunately unnecessary (since it would be tedious) to enter into a detailed examination of the deceased Charles Povey's affairs. The simple fact is that they had proved perplexed in a degree not anticipated by his hopeful brother (and supplanter) when weighing his future chances amid the solitude of the Pacific Ocean. A blessed innocence, he now knew, had been his companion on board the *Gay Phoenix*.

He had never, it was true, thought of Charles as other than a bit of a rascal. Rascality, after all, ran in the Povey blood. Even the musical Povey, founder of the family's fortunes, had distinguishably had his shady aspect. Arthur had been acute enough to scent that. Nevertheless Povey Senior had kept on the right side of the law. He had been an Alderman; he had been the Master of a Livery Company;

his name had been much in demand as a director of the most respectable concerns. But Charles was different. Even at the height of his success (so tragically cut short by that clout on the head) such accolades had somehow eluded him. For years—to put it brutally—he couldn't have known quite what was going to catch up on him. And then he had died— and Arthur had stepped into his increasingly pinching shoes. Butter, equally with his patron, had found himself accepting this inheritance. Their joint lives had become, in the main, a succession of holding operations, each tumbling on the other. Butter—to his credit be it said—seemed to enjoy this posture of affairs more than Povey did.

'That damned ring-fence,' Povey said when his butler had withdrawn from the dining-room, '—I don't see the sense of it. It's going up in absurd patches; it's grotesquely obtrusive; and it wouldn't keep out a cat.'

'It isn't meant to, old cock.' Butter—or Bread—had preserved the very bad habit of offensively familiar address to his employer as soon as they were alone. 'It's the image that counts. For you have to face it, you know. Your honey-moon period is over. The money's there—or in a short-term way it's there—but you'll revel in it only in remote corners of the globe. A dash to your private jet and a month's riotous living at Montego Bay : that's you now, my boy. Otherwise, it's the recluse, and with the accent on a dash of dottiness behind it. The remote control going yet remoter still. Be-come a legend in that way, and you may survive into a green old age. Muck around, run into somebody who suspects something, and you're a goner, my lad. It's as simple as that.'

'Then you'll be a goner too.'

'In a different sense, I hope.' And Butter produced his irritating wicked grin. 'Over the hills and far away : that will be yours truly.'

Povey allowed himself a snarl. It was becoming his answer to the grin. Intermittently at least, he was inclined to recall with resentment the manner in which Butter had first imposed their partnership upon him. On the other hand, their curious nocturnal adventure, and the change of heart which had accompanied it on his own part, seemed to have produced a genuine affection of sorts in Butter. Should a crash come, it was certainly true that Butter would bolt if he could. But Povey accepted this as quite in line with his own vision of things, and on the whole their failures in accord didn't last long. It was in what might be termed no more than a key of minor discontent that Povey spoke next.

'That woman you told me about,' he said. 'I don't think you should have set the dogs on her.'

'I didn't. I just had them accompany us to the front door. You wouldn't have had me waste time on her and her idiot son, would you?'

'He really is an idiot?'

'Completely moronic. His attempts at talk don't come to more than a kind of slobbering.'

'There was never anything of that sort in the family.'

'Well, that's a confession, that is.' Butter was amused. 'Ought I to have welcomed him home? Or turned over the family jewels to his ma?'

'Of course not. But it's devilish awkward, people remembering that sort of thing about Charles. And I expect others will turn up. This whole plan has been a mistake, if you ask me. It's running my head into a noose, coming back to Brockholes.'

'It's nothing of the kind. It's good psychology, my boy, or I'd never have thought it up. Buying the old Povey home and settling in is the one thing no impostor would ever dream of. And it's good for your ego, too.'

'I can't say I feel it that way.' Arthur Povey brooded darkly, and for several minutes, indeed, seemed to lose himself in a deep absence of mind. 'And he's *not* my child!' he suddenly shouted strangely.

'What's that?' Butter (now Bread) sat up abruptly on his chair.

'I say there's no real reason to suppose this Corp woman's imbecile is Charles's son at all.' Povey had looked momentarily bewildered. 'It's an impudent imposture.'

'Well, you're an authority on that.' Butter eyed his employer narrowly. 'Are you sure you're all right?' he asked.

'Of course I'm all right. And then there was this man you say called himself Appleby. I don't like the sound of him.'

'That's a different matter. No more do I.'

'Some sort of local squire, you say. But I don't remember any Applebys in these parts. And I would, if they were really in that walk of life.'

'No reason why you should. He's a newcomer, comparatively speaking. But *I* remembered him. Recognized him at once.' Butter paused warily; he had a stiff new fence to get over in vindicating his competent handling of things. 'He ran the London fuzz, old boy. When he retired he was their bloody top man.'

'Good God, *that* Appleby!' Povey was aghast. 'I've heard of *him*, all right. What's he doing, nosing round here?'

'Nothing very much, I'd say. But I looked him up as soon as he went away. Long ago, he married a woman who inherited a place called Long Dream Manor. Name of Raven.'

'Well, I'm damned!' Povey was as astonished as alarmed. 'I remember *them*, although we didn't know them very well. All as mad as hatters. And *they* ran to morons quite often, people said. It was a Raven father that boy had, if you ask me! What the hell was this fellow doing, poking in pretty well the moment we've arrived? And what the hell did you mean yattering to him? He was the one to set the dogs at.'

'Come, come—no panic, old cock.' Butter, if not quite at ease, spoke in easy tones. 'He's the very man to feed the story to. The last man anybody would think could have any wool pulled over his eyes. So just pull it, good and hearty, and you've played a trump card.'

'Which is more psychology, I suppose.' Povey, before whom stood a decanter of port, applied himself nervously to this refreshment. 'You spotted Appleby. What about Appleby spotting you?'

'Well, there's the rub, I'm free to own. I don't think he did. But he may have.' For a moment Butter, too, brooded. Then his natural resilience triumphed. 'I've been quite a famous man in my day, you know. Almost in the big time, you might say. Before undeserved misfortune overtook me.'

'It's dam' well a deserved misfortune that may be coming your way now, Butter. I don't like this, at all. It's a shock to me. It gives me that nasty feeling of an empty bit in my head.'

'I don't want to hear any more about that empty bit in your head, Mr Charles Povey of Brockholes Abbey. It's not wholesome, that kind of thinking.'

'And after a bloody bad day.'

'What do you mean—a bloody bad day?' Butter was startled. 'I told you you oughtn't to go mucking off to London. That's unwholesome too. All those business satraps of yours'—this was a flash of Butter the scholar—'are contacted only through yours truly. That's the drill. The mystery man of Brockholes runs his bleeding empire only through me. You've taken to abstruse studies, you have. And dreaming up large schemes of philanthropy.' Butter paused. 'Just what happened?' he demanded savagely.

'It may be nothing. It's only that a lot of them seem to want to clear out. A lot of those new chaps we put in when we fired the old ones. Something's changing in them. Keen as mustard, weren't they, at first? As they bloody well should be, on three times the salary they ever touched before. Do you know how it seems to me? They've heard something. That's it.'

*   *   *

Butter got up and walked to the door of the dining-room. An old instinct was suddenly alive in him. He opened the door abruptly, but there was nobody there.

'This sort of talk,' he said, returning to the table, 'ought to be kept for when you and me are walking round your ancestral estate. With nobody listening except your bleeding pedigree herd.'

'I haven't got a bleeding pedigree herd.'

'Yes, you have. I've bought you one.' Butter's grin had returned. 'Stock-breeding. That's one of your absorbing ploys now. Not the Stock Exchange, old cock, but improving your country's livestock. It's a most gentlemanly thing.'

'Gentlemanlike,' Povey said automatically. He had formed the habit of correcting Butter's minor solecisms. 'We just don't know enough,' he added.

'If you're sufficiently nippy,' Butter said cheerfully, 'a little goes a long way. Still, I wouldn't mind filling up the dossier on that brother of yours, I must say. You ought to remember more about him than you do.'

'About who?' Perhaps because he had now drunk a good deal of port, Povey looked vaguely confused.

'About Charles. Why can't you listen to me?'

'Yes, of course. Charles.' Povey nodded vigorously. 'Charles,' he repeated.

Butter consulted his own glass. There were moments, he might have been reflecting, in which something demonstrably odd was going on in his employer's mind.

'For instance,' he went on, 'who did Charles mean to leave his money to?'

'Not to me—or we shouldn't be in just this position now.' Arthur Povey chuckled; he was again entirely alert. 'He did once say an uncommonly queer thing. There mightn't be a penny for anybody, he said. Not enough to start a cat-and-dog home.'

'Charles said that?' Setting down his glass, Butter frowned.

'He just meant, I suppose, that he was in a good many pretty risky enterprises. We've discovered that, all right.'

'We certainly have. But do you know what I sometimes think?' Povey looked moodily at his assistant. 'I think he may have been aware of the possibility of a very big crash indeed. And if it was coming to him then, it may be coming to me now.'

'What do you mean—a very big crash?'

'Suppose we're not just involved with phoney affairs as often as not. That sort of thing can be coped with easily enough. You just turn on those accountants and people to mix up this and that—and long before the mess can be unscrambled you've made your own get-away from it.' It was with an effect of considerable lucidity that Povey thus expounded the elements of company finance. 'But suppose that the whole show hinges on a single colossal fraud? One's heard of such things. Something so simple that it went like a bomb from the start. But so simple, too, that the whole show will be given away instantly if somebody just happens to open the right drawer. I sometimes dream about that. The chap going to the right drawer.'

'You're fancying things, old cock. Always your trouble, that is. One day, you'll get matters badly wrong.' Butter for a moment looked frankly troubled. 'I've got to keep an eye on you, I have,' he added broodingly.

'It would bust me in a day. I'd wake up, and—just as Charles said—there wouldn't be a penny.'

'There'd be a copper, old boy.' Butter seemed cheered up by this grim joke. 'Waiting at the bedside with the bracelets. And then, Squire Povey, you'd spend months being hustled in and out of a Crown Court with a blanket over your head.' Butter paused. 'Probably a smelly one,' he added brutally.

'Then there's Charles's private life.' Povey had ignored these pleasantries. 'This woman Corp brings *that* up.'

'You're going morbid, you are. Who cares about the

Corps? What if there are half a dozen crazy women around, thinking to father their bastards on you? It's still an English gentleman's privilege, that. To scatter his Maker's image o'er the land, as some long-haired character put it.' Butter was plainly delighted at displaying this reach of literary reference. 'If you were a bit of a lad in your youth, Mr Charles Povey as now is, the locals will only think the better of you.' Butter announced this with the conviction of one who commands a clear view of English society in the twentieth century. 'Mind you, I don't say it wouldn't cost you a tenner now and then,' he added humorously. 'But scattering tenners o'er the land is quite your forte, if I remember aright.'

'I wish you'd go to hell!' It was wholly unfavourably that Povey had responded to this facetious reminiscence. 'What do I know what Charles may have done? He had a violent streak in him. All the Poveys have a violent streak—and that's something you'd better remember. That I have it myself, Butter.' Arthur Povey gulped down more port—being perhaps a little taken aback at having inadvertently uttered this threat. 'I wouldn't have chopped off Charles's finger in the wood-shed otherwise.'

'Well, well—here's a revelation!' Butter was delighted. 'Sometimes I admire you—Mr Arthur Povey that was. And you made amends, didn't you, on board that blessed yacht? An eye for an eye, as the Good Book says.'

'Shut your silly mouth!' This further and profane joke had very properly offended Povey. 'It's a nightmare, I tell you, what I may have inherited from Charles, one way and another. I ought to have thought about it.'

'It's no use crying over spilt milk—or fingers either.'

'I don't like your tone, Butter. All this isn't funny.'

'We'd better see it as funny. Keeps the spirits up. That's—'

'Psychology, I suppose.' Povey uttered these words on an

injudicious shout—a circumstance underlined by the fact that the butler had just entered the room with coffee. Povey watched him come and go with understandable impatience. 'And all those servants,' he resumed querulously. 'Who the devil are they? Why do we need them? I don't like their looks at all. You hired them. Where do they come from?'

'They're old friends of mine.' Butter made this shocking revelation composedly. 'Your butler's on parole, as a matter of fact. A gentleman has to have an establishment. But don't you worry. I have tabs on the lot. There won't be any trouble there.'

'You mean you've filled this house with a pack of gaol-birds?'

'Not a pack. Birds don't go in packs. Say a flock of them. Nice people, really.'

'They'll spy on me.'

'Nobody will spy on you. Or not in the house. There was a spy of sorts in the park this afternoon.'

'What's that?' Povey seemed to find this an even greater shock than the discovery that his new servants were recruited exclusively from the criminal classes. 'What sort of spy?'

'A pretty inefficient one, old boy. But it was a rum thing. Just after I'd got rid of those Corps, I happened to look out of the window of my office. You haven't seen that yet, but it's going to be very snug. And a nice bit of afternoon sun.'

'Damn the afternoon sun! Go on.'

'There's a scrap of woodland, and just in front of it there was an odd sort of stump I hadn't noticed before. Then a woman appeared, and chucked a stone or something—'

'What sort of woman?'

'I haven't a clue. It was a fair way off, you see. She chucked a stone, and out came a man with a pair of binoculars slung round his neck. They had a word together, and the woman marched off. Then the chap packed up, and went off too. He'd been spying, all right, and this woman had caught him out.'

'She wasn't one of those precious servants of yours?'

'Not a bit. The sort of person who might have been coming to tea, with you, old boy. As I said, quite a rum go altogether.'

There was silence for a moment, as Arthur Povey contemplated these facts. It looked as if the more he contemplated them the less he liked them, for he might have been observed to be turning positively pale.

'Perhaps,' he said on a note of momentary hope, 'he was just planning a common burglary.'

'Very probably. With an eye on the family Caravaggio.'

'There isn't a family Caravaggio.'

'Yes, there is—or there's going to be. I've bought you one. It will arrive with the pedigree herd.'

'I've listened to enough of your nonsense for tonight, Butter.' Povey got to his feet. It was quite likely, he reflected, that there really were such purchases coming along. Their absurdity would gratify Butter's freakish sense of humour— in addition to which he would no doubt have arranged himself a substantial rake-off.

'Very well.' Butter had some appearance of being genuinely offended. 'I'll offer you a dozen words of cold sense instead, Povey. It *is* tricky. It's tricky all round. And I've been hearing things, I have. I've had my ear to the ground— and others' ears too. Why did your brother go on that last long cruise with you? Maybe he liked that sort of thing. But it was convenient as well.'

'Convenient?'

'Now, just you listen. I've spared you, I have. Your nerves aren't too good. But I'll tell you now. There were those that were gunning for him. Literally, Arthur Povey. And they're gunning for him now. How do I know, you ask? It's because I have my methods—that's what it is. So you do as I tell you, see? Without fail, and every time. That's your best chance, Mr Charles-Arthur or Arthur-Charles.'

As this speech progressed, Povey's pollar had taken on a greenish tinge. In his rational mind he dimly knew that Butter might well be lying; once or twice before, his self-appointed secretary had unmasked this kind of battery; had thus, as it were, tightened the screw. But for the moment Povey was bowled over. He had a sense of unknown dangers assailing him on every hand. He bitterly rued that mad hour on the broad waters of the Pacific Ocean. He had bitten off enormously more than he could chew. He felt—it was almost like a moment's hysteria—that all was lost.

'Curse you,' Arthur Povey cried, 'and curse the lot of them!' And he waved his fists in air, much in the manner of a villain in Victorian melodrama. 'But they shan't catch me—never! They shan't get me down!' He was glaring at Butter much as the unfortunate Doctor Faustus might have glared at Mephistopheles. 'Not as long as I know a way out!'

'Well, well!' Butter (now Bread) broke into brutal laughter. 'The dishonoured squire retreats to the barn with his shot-gun, and a dull report follows.' He grinned at Povey, who stared back at him blankly—so that an exact observer might have detected that some curious misapprehension had arisen between these two closely confabulating men. 'No, no, old cock,' Butter continued. 'It won't do. The death of Brutus, eh? Povey the noblest Roman of them all. It's very pretty on the stage, but it's futile in real life. It isn't on, suicide isn't. And I tell you why. It gets you nowhere.'

The felicitousness of this last expression (carrying, as it did, a sardonic implication of which Mephistopheles himself might not have been ashamed) was unfortunately lost on Arthur Povey. He was engaged in recollecting himself, in pulling himself together. His outcry represented an aberration of a sort most urgently demanding to be controlled—

and he was uneasily aware of himself as perhaps increasingly liable to fly off the handle from time to time. It was largely Butter's fault; he was a most irritating man. But there was no question of Butter being expendable. Realizing this, Arthur Povey made his peace with him now. They were an isolated couple, after all, sharing a secret known to nobody else in the world. Both knew that, if they didn't manage to be companionable on the whole, only chaos could succeed. It was in tacit acknowledgement of this fact of life that the two men consumed a good deal of brandy together before going to bed.

IX

BUTTER, IT HAS been remarked, may well not have been telling the truth in declaring that dire enemies of the late Charles Povey, unaware of his being beyond the reach of vengeance, were abroad in the land. Butter may simply have been contriving a malign fiction, designed to demoralize Arthur Povey and thus increase his ascendancy over his employer. But however this may have been, he was certainly not wrong in asserting that Arthur Povey, at least for some time ahead, had no alternative to accepting a stiff seclusion as his present way of life.

Povey had, indeed, been right—brilliantly right—in guessing that great enterprises could be run by an invisible man, and large revenues, as a result, be appropriated for his use. His cables, his telephone-calls, his brother's scrawled signatures on a cheque or other document : it was plain that nobody sensed the slightest need to question these. One simple assumption of his false identity at the start had done the whole trick, and on the business side of things there hadn't been a hitch. There had of course been, and there would continue to be, occasions upon which a personal appearance by the mystery man was essential. But these were in the main formal occasions round a table, arranged at the behest of equally eminent tycoons from other countries. They were all a sort of people who constantly moved from capital to capital, continent to continent, in luxuriously appointed private aeroplanes. They ate and drank a great deal; such mental clarity as survived their way of life was wholly concentrated upon the complex financial documents thrust under their nose by high-powered bankers and accountants and managers; they hadn't the slightest interest in each other as human beings. Charles Povey as a kind of faceless man of legendary elusiveness and taciturnity, broodingly aloof until he snapped out some decision and departed, suited them very well. They admired his impersonal style, and sometimes even resolved to imitate it. Unless (as Povey, indeed, had increasing reason to fear) something very irregular indeed began to be insistently heard as at the heart, as constituting the very pulse, of the Povey empire, he was tolerably secure for a long time ahead.

Where he had gone wrong was in over-estimating the advantage he must gain from the glimpsed tenuousness and discontinuousness of his brother's private life. The world was full of people who remembered Charles Povey perfectly well, who were interested in continuing to know him, who cherished plans for contacting him again in the interest of one hopeful design or another. It was this that made Arthur's frequentation of fashionable resorts, expensive courtesans (in fact pretty well everything that makes life glorious) perpetually hazardous. Almost every sort of planned and foreseen encounter could be handled. But he was perpetually at the mercy of chance.

Perhaps Butter, too, hadn't at first quite the measure of this. But he was right on the ball now, and had swiftly planned the measures necessary for survival. Povey was only beginning to glimpse how Draconian they were going to be. His virtual immurement in this beastly Brockholes Abbey of his childhood looked like being the cardinal point in Butter's design. Povey was himself going to become a kind of latter day *moine malgré lui*—the sole member of an order closed and sealed off within the bounds of his own cloister. It was a perfectly nightmarish prospect.

All this was going gloomily through Povey's head as he breakfasted in solitude on the following morning. (He had at least managed to be firm about not starting the day in

Butter's company.) But at the moment the effect of seclusion didn't extend beyond the room in which he was being served. Elsewhere there was a lot of noise going on. In fact the house could be said to be humming with life. This effect didn't proceed from its new domestic staff, which had on the whole the unobtrusiveness of persons professionally habituated to going about their activities quietly and unobserved. It was due to the fact there were still workmen of various sorts all over the place. This in itself didn't annoy Povey. If he had to live at Brockholes as if it were the Castle of Chillon or some such place of dismal incarceration the dilapidated dump might as well be made tolerably smart and comfortable. What did disturb him was having been hustled into it so hastily, so that a smell of wet paint was mingling with that of his grilled kidneys now and he couldn't move down a corridor without tumbling over somebody laying carpets.

In any circumstances all this would have been disagreeable to Povey, since he attached importance to maintaining, on land as at sea, a ship-shape state of affairs around him. But what really bothered him was the haste with which Butter had huddled him into the house. Butter was tiresomely inclined to jeer at him as prone to panic, but this precipitate retreat looked very much like the work of one who was panicking himself. Perhaps Butter really did know more than he had told about some gathering storm.

But another thought now struck Povey. That there were people actually gunning for *him* (or for Charles, as they imagined him to be) was an assertion for which he had only Butter's word; mere exposure in his imposture was his only certain and assured danger, and it was at least less alarming than the thought of enemies pursuing some obscure and potentially lethal personal vendetta. But people had really been gunning for Butter, and with the most nakedly homicidal intent. Their joint seaside adventure authenticated that. So wasn't this hastily contrived Fortress Brockholes effect perhaps more in aid of Butter than of himself?

Povey found himself not particularly keen to follow up this kind of thinking. Being an intelligent man, he had come to recognize the danger inherent in building up a resentful attitude towards his associate; just let that get out of hand and they would both be in the soup. And Butter, after all, was also one of God's creatures (although not so important and deserving a specimen as Arthur Povey) and entitled to play for his own hand. Taking this enlightened and humane view of the matter now, Povey did his best to thrust hostile impulses out of his head, and sought distraction in taking a prowl through his new and contracted empire. So might Satan, cast from the empyrean, have prowled the sad variety of hell, or the Emperor Napoleon have perambulated bits and pieces of the forty-seven square miles of St Helena.

The various tradesmen presently employed in the house were clearly from reputable firms, accustomed to labour for the better ease and amenity of the gentry. Recognizing in Povey the lord of the manor, they comported themselves respectfully as he roamed around. This was soothing. So, in a way, was the lavishness of what was being done. The bills would be enormous, and Povey actually took a sardonic satisfaction in the thought that, if a sudden crash did come, none of them was likely to be paid. He was startled only when he reached the drawing-room, which was the principal apartment in the house. It was being decorated as if in the expectation that he would here entertain the remaining Crowned Heads of Europe or of the globe. Butter—it was all, of course, of Butter's planning—had really gone to town. (The phrase momentarily vexed Povey, who had been pretty well told, after yesterday's expedition, that he was not himself going to be allowed to go to town again.)

From floor to ceiling, there was clearly to be a grand and

unifying design, and it was being achieved under the super-intendence of a female, who was even now marching round the room in a commanding way. Povey saw at once that she was of what might be called the *cordon bleu* type. Her fees would be unblushingly on the scale of a top surgeon's or portrait-painter's. And she would expect to be treated as one treats an artist or architect of the first eminence. Povey, a polite man, an English gentleman of the old school, realized that it was very improper in him not even to know her name.

This difficulty was in his head when the female turned to him with a brisk good-morning. Of course *she* knew who *he* was. And suddenly a shocking thing happened. She was regarding him mischievously and in a manner to be charac-terized as wholly unprofessional. It was instantly and abund-antly clear that she expected to be recognized.

It was a difficult situation, and by no means unprecedented. Here, in fact, was the recurrent crisis, the ever-threatening moment of truth. Povey understood this at once. What it took further seconds for him to grasp was the character of the relationship which this person had undoubtedly enjoyed with his brother. Her charms were mature, but they were still staggering. It was not mere dismay that was making Arthur Povey's head swim.

'Charles, darling, I could hardly wait. It was a most mar-vellous surprise!'

'Yes,' Povey said feebly. 'I suppose so.'

'Of course, I'd never been to Brockholes, and I don't think you ever mentioned it. So when that nice man told me your name, and how you wanted me to accept the com-mission, I was struck all of a heap. I'd felt, you know, that you weren't terribly interested in me any longer. After all, it's been years and years.'

'So it has. One does lose touch. I've travelled a good deal, you know. And business has been very absorbing.'

'It has been flourishing, it seems.' The female glanced round the splendours she was being required to summon into being. 'You've been soaring, Charles. And how wonderful to be back in your old home! Mr Bread has explained it all to me.'

'Not quite all, I expect. And you seem to have been doing rather well in your own profession yourself.' He was about to add, 'If it *is* your profession,' but judged that the joke might not be well received. Here, certainly, was one of those top tarts with accounts of whom Charles had been accustomed to torment him. And he wasn't quite sure of the conversational tone which gentlemen adopt to such ladies when according them protection. His own experience was limited. He'd had his day, of course; he'd had quite a lot of days during the all too brief period in which he had believed his imposture so secure that he could live a life of care-free indulgence in the hot spots of Europe. But he hadn't quite the touch—if that was the word—of a man long habituated to that purple. Still, it shouldn't be difficult to hit the right note. The urgent difficulty was that he hadn't a notion what to call the woman. He looked wildly round as if for inspiration. Perhaps 'darling' would do once or twice—he was holding it in reserve— but if he couldn't put a real name to her pretty soon he was sunk. Or was he? Perhaps she would merely conclude that he recognized her only as one of such a large crowd of houris whose favours he had enjoyed that her name simply wasn't lodged in his head. In that case, she might be offended, change her line, fall back on being merely a professional adviser. That, indeed, would be the safest way to try to play it.

He became aware that he oughtn't to be looking round at all; that it was ungallant to do other than let his gaze be riveted by the charms immediately before him. Being a man of address, he coped with this bad behaviour at once.

'It's perfectly gorgeous,' he said, with a wave at the transformed drawing-room. 'But not nearly as gorgeous as you, my darling.'

These were fateful words; they represented a kind of burning of boats. The woman *was* a houri, and Povey's impulse to play safe had deserted him. He had been, after all, on what might coarsely be called sexual short-commons for some time. And now he noticed that they were standing close to a writing-table at which it appeared this dangerous charmer had set up her working quarters. It was covered with a litter of papers and sketches.

'Are those your designs?' he asked with a great appearance of eagerness. 'May I look at them?'

'Of course, Charles darling. They're all yours, aren't they?'

At this, Povey went up to the table, and immediately saw that his genius had been vindicated. There was, among the rest of the stuff, a little pile of writing-paper, and it bore a printed letter-head. He squinted at this and read:

PERPETUA PORTER
Interior Decoration and Design

'And is that going to be the carpet?' Povey pointed more or less at random at one drawing. 'I can hardly wait to see it. Your taste is as marvellous as ever, Perpetua my love.'

'Perpetua?' Miss (or Mrs) Porter pouted. 'Isn't that rather formal, Charles? You always called me Pops.'

'Pops, of course.' Povey judged this a revolting pet name for any woman, but managed to articulate it fondly and (what wasn't easy) on a kind of amorous dying fall.

'Sweet, sweet Charles—it's fabulous to have found you again.'

'Yes, isn't it? Me to have found you, I mean.' There being

no workmen close by, Povey took Pops's hand familiarly and gave it a little squeeze. There had come to him the amazing fact that this stunning woman had not only been infatuated with Charles at some unknown past time; she was infatuated with the person she supposed to be Charles now. *Agnosco* —she might have been saying with poor old Dido or who- ever—*veteris vestigia flammae*. He had only to put out his hand again—in a more definitive manner, this time—and the thing was in the bag. 'Pops, darling,' he said, 'it's a lovely morning. Shall we go out into the park?'

'Yes, Charles my sweet, do let's. And we can have a splendid chat about old times.'

'So we can.' Povey's enthusiasm was not immediate. 'You can tell me all about yourself,' he added. 'Everything you've been doing all this time. I'd love to hear it.'

'So you shall. And you'll tell me everything too. I've ever so many things to ask you.'

'Or perhaps all that can keep, Pops darling. There are times—aren't there?—when deeds are sweeter than words.'

'Darling, that's just the kind of thing you used to say.'

'Well, then—now for the kind of thing I used to do.'

Thus, with incredible rashness, the commonly so wary Arthur Povey—fondly overcome with female charm.

X

H E   W A S   T O wonder afterwards whether she had known
all the time; whether she hadn't in the very moment of first
glimpsing him in the drawing-room seen who he wasn't and
who he must be. If this were so, she was a thoroughly malicious as well as vicious woman, since she had hoarded her
knowledge in order to deploy it in a strikingly wounding
way. For she had simply sat up on the grass (he had found
a sunny but secluded little glade), stretched, yawned,
smoothed her hair with the prescriptive automatic hand, and
pronounced lazily certain ingeniously lacerating words.

'That was quite nice, my dear man. But not nearly so
nice as with Charles Povey.'

He had stared at her blankly. Seconds before, he had been
conscious only of appropriately languorous ease, and now he
hadn't ceased staring at her in a stupid incomprehension
when she spoke again.

'So you must be Charles's wet brother.' (She certainly had
the air of having arrived at this conclusion only within the
last few minutes.) 'Is that right?'

'What do you mean—Charles's wet brother?' As he
uttered these words Povey was aware of them as singularly
futile and feeble. He was going to do even worse than when
first unmasked by Butter.

'It's what he always called you. He didn't seem to like you
very much.'

'I didn't like him.' Povey had decided that deception was
useless. Perhaps he could presently strangle Perpetua Porter,
and put the blame on somebody like Mrs Corp's imbecile

son. But for the moment frankness was the thing—frankness and playing it cool.

'Neither did I, as a matter of fact.' Pops spoke as if her new lover had gained considerable ground with her. 'Of course I could put on a turn for him. A girl has to be able to do that. You saw me at it.'

'I certainly did, Pops.' Povey had been rather struck by Miss Porter's 'girl'. It somehow suggested quite humble beginnings in the less socially esteemed of her professions. He wondered about the other one. She had clearly achieved some standing in this decorating and designing nonsense; even if some benevolent admirer had set her up in it she must be pretty smart to hold her own in a crowded field. And Butter must have heard well of her before taking her on. It must be a precarious living, all the same. For a moment Povey felt almost sympathetically disposed towards the lady. When he spoke, however, it was with an air of greater friendliness than he actually felt. Those first words he had spoken after what had seemed to him a creditable performance were still rankling a good deal.

'Look here!' he said urgently. 'Aren't you kidding? Didn't you spot I wasn't Charles at once—just as soon, I mean, as we met in that drawing-room?'

'Really and truly not, darling. I may still call you darling? But I do know your real name. Charles mentioned it several times. It's Arthur.'

'Yes, it's Arthur.'

'I must say you're terribly like Charles. You speak like him, and move like him. So I don't think you'll do badly at whatever little game you're up to.' Miss Porter offered all these observations in a commendatory tone. Then she laughed—robustly and not particularly kindly. 'Only I think you must be careful about going to bed—or into this very nice park—with *any* of Charles's old lady friends. In fact, and to be quite frank, I'd strongly advise going to work elsewhere.' Miss Porter paused thoughtfully. 'Do you know? It's been just like something in the Bible.'

'What the devil do you mean by that?'

'Don't you remember? "The voice is Jacob's voice, but the hands are the hands of Esau." And it's about stealing a birthright, or something.'

Povey ought perhaps to have been edified by this evidence of his companion's unexpected command of Holy Writ. But in fact he was extremely shocked, and his flicker of kindly feeling for her faded. He found himself, indeed, grinding his teeth and much inclined to take an immediate swipe at her. Folk-tales, he was recalling, have frequent recourse to what literary historians call the Bed Trick, and he seemed rather to remember that Shakespeare himself makes use of it at least twice. You get into bed with a woman in the dark, and she quite fails to tumble to the fact that you aren't somebody else. Of course with Pops there hadn't been a bed, and it hadn't been dark either. His vanity was quite acutely injured, all the same. Pops hadn't ceased to be extremely desirable. But he was absolutely certain he was never going to *like* her again. As he was now in her power, this seemed an unfortunate thing.

'And I wonder what you *are* up to,' Pops said thoughtfully. She was gazing out over the park as she spoke—but it was absently, and as if she were surveying a prospect she couldn't yet clearly define. 'Does Mr Bread know?' she asked.

'His name isn't Bread. That's just one of his silly jokes. It's Butter. He says he knows which side his bread's buttered on. Butter's always making idiotic cracks. And yes—he does know.'

'Does anybody else know?'

'No, nobody.' Povey weighed his words. 'It's just us three,' he said. 'We might be described as in it together.'

'What fun! I suppose you murdered Charles? He *was* rather a pig.'

'I did nothing of the kind!' Arthur Povey was horrified. He was also frightened. Strangely enough, it had never occurred to him that, if he were one day exposed, this calm assumption of Miss Porter's might well become the conclusion of the law.

'But he is dead?'

'Yes, he is dead.' Povey persevered in his resolution to be candid. He had to face it : he was back on Square One. His next move, he supposed, must be to suggest that suitcase stuffed with ten-pound notes.

'There's an awful lot of money?'

'Quite a lot.'

'And is your friend Bread in on the thing for his health?'

'Butter. And you might say he's in on it for the jam.' Povey thought a tone of mild gamesomeness might suggest he was effortlessly keeping his end up. He was badly in need of time in which to plan a course of action in facing this hideous new threat. 'It's a long story,' he added lightly and vaguely.

'You'll have to tell it to me.'

Povey didn't at all like the way Miss Porter said this. There was a hint of command in it. In Butter he already had one master; it looked as if here was another. Or rather it looked as if here was a mistress in both senses of the word. He much doubted whether his possession of her in the one sense (even if it continued) would make up for her possession of him in the other.

'I'll be delighted to tell you the whole thing,' he said. 'But, oddly enough, it mayn't be easy. You see, it's largely lost through something queer that's happened to my memory. What the doctors call amnesia.'

'Arthur, darling, don't make me laugh.' Pops uttered this demotic formula for incredulity with considerable force.

'Well, now, that's just it.' Povey took one of his rash intuitive plunges. 'You're certain that I'm Arthur Povey. So am I—just at the moment. But not always. Sometimes I'm not pretending to be Charles. I *am* Charles.'

'That's absolute rubbish.' Miss Porter was plainly shaken. 'Such a thing just couldn't happen.'

'There, I assure you, you're quite wrong, Pops. I've read it all up.'

'Trust you for that. You're cunning, Arthur Povey. It makes me feel I might do worse than come in on the act.'

'You'd have to be invited, my dear.' Povey spoke with a robustness he didn't feel. 'But as I was saying. I've read all about the psychology of imposture. Butter talks a lot about psychology, but hardly has a notion of what the word means, the low bastard.' Povey checked himself in this irrelevant expression of feeling. 'Impostors do sometimes come to believe in their own imposture. Lambert Simnel, Perkin Warbeck : people of that sort.'

'I've never heard of them. But that must be when there's some real mystery about their birth or origins.'

'Yes, in a way.' Povey realized that Pops, although not perhaps extensively educated, owned a strong natural intelligence. 'But, in that case, they're not strictly impostors. They're claimants or pretenders, on the strength of evidence that can be read one way or another. And I repeat the plain fact that sometimes I *am* Charles. I find myself— although usually not for more than minutes at a time— puzzled by what Butter is saying to me. You see, it all began, or all but began, in a very confused way.'

'When you believe you're Charles what do you believe about Arthur?'

Povey blinked and hesitated. He found this question— which again testified to the sharpness of Miss Porter's wits— obscure and difficult.

'I think I believe he died at sea.'

146

'You're at sea yourself, if you ask me.' Miss Porter stared seriously at her new and problematical lover. She seemed disposed to acquit him of mere imbecile fabrication. 'Does Butter know all about this complication?'

'I sometimes feel he suspects it. I come out with silly remarks about the inside of my head. But I haven't confided in him.'

'As you have in me, darling.' Miss Porter, perhaps significantly, had returned for the first time to this familiar endearment. 'Which is quite right, of course. I'm the natural person for that. Or I'm going to be.'

'You're going to be?' Povey, in his turn, stared seriously at his newly acquired mistress, but it was a stare tinged with a fresh alarm. Dimly, he knew what she was driving at.

'Of course, I needn't *know*. I needn't be known to know, that is. If there was a crash, I could still be in the clear.'

'You're an unscrupulous little bitch.' A tinge of admiration infused this judgement.

'Well, darling, it does look as if a good deal of unscrupulousness has to be the order of the day all round, doesn't it?' And suddenly Miss Porter laughed her clear unkindly laugh again. 'Can you tell me—but, of course, I'd have to consult lawyers in a discreet way—just how marriage settlements and things are affected by bankruptcies?' Pops paused. 'And other misfortunes?'

'I don't know what you're talking about.'

'Don't be feeble, Arthur. Of course you do. And we mustn't waste time. The first point is how to handle Butter.'

'Butter isn't easy to handle. He has a flair, curse him, for doing the handling himself.'

'Yes, do let's curse him. But think of a little action as well. Our engagement had better be private for a start.'

'Our engagement?'

'In fact until after the wedding. And you must get a special licence at once. I think it's from the Archbishop of

Canterbury. But you mustn't be too frank with him. He probably has rather strict ideas, wouldn't you say? About people knowing who they really are, and so on.'

And now it had all come home to Arthur Povey. The woman was going to be a life sentence—which was probably a bit more than even convicted imposters receive in court. He remembered with a sudden chill that, although known as Pops among her intimates, Perpetua was her actual name.

PART FOUR

Speculations of a Policeman in Retirement

XI

'I HOPE THE church sale was the usual enormous success?'

The Applebys had been abroad for some months, and Judith was conscientiously catching up on the local news. This was her first luncheon party since getting back. There were only three guests: Dr Dunton and Colonel and Mrs Birch-Blackie. An elderly lady had cried off at the last moment on account of a sudden and alarming indisposition which had befallen an equally elderly horse.

'Just over three hundred pounds,' Dr Dunton said. 'By no means a record, but a most satisfactory sum nevertheless. And the day was fortunately fine. Nothing but your own absence, Lady Appleby, clouded the general enjoyment.'

'Quite right, Padre,' Colonel Birch-Blackie said. 'Dashed good. Jolly neat.' Colonel Birch-Blackie, although not intellectually distinguished, was a wholly amiable man. 'Amazing lot of things for sale. Found I'd bought a pair of bed-socks. Thought they were something for polishing a car. Gave them to our cook. Woman with uncommonly large feet.'

'Although I ought honestly to mention,' Dr Dunton pursued, 'that there was one somewhat untoward incident. However, it was quickly over. And one can't really blame the old man, considering that he is so far advanced within the vale of years. Moreover, I may well have committed an error of judgement in making the arrangement I did. It was designed as a composing and harmonizing gesture, and I fear that it misfired. I hadn't realized the strength of latent feeling in the parish. Had you been available, Lady Appleby, I should, of course, have consulted you in the first instance,

151

and the momentary embarrassment might have been obviated. However—and as I say—I don't reproach old Mr Hoobin. The behaviour of Mrs Corp was undoubtedly provocative.'

'Hoobin?' Appleby explained. 'Good heavens! What has the wretched dotard done? Publicly walloped his unfortunate nephew for filching from the bun-and-cake stall?'

'Nothing of the sort—although it is true that Solo Hoobin must be described as having been to some extent involved. The senior Hoobin's action amounted to a kind of testifying before the congregation. It was triggered off, as they now say, by the spectacle presented by Sammy Corp. But I see, my dear Appleby, that a more orderly exposition of the unfortunate incident is required.'

'Dashed good idea,' Colonel Birch-Blackie said. 'Found it a bit bewildering myself, I'm bound to own. Distracting, too. Probably why I bought those damned bed-socks. I've always said a fellow needs all his wits about him at a church sale. Once thought I was buying a bottle of Jerry Linger's port dirt cheap at a couple of quid. Being his nobs and his lordship in these parts, old Jerry feels, you know, that he must turn in something with a bit of class to it. Damned bottle proved to be old Mrs Somebody's rhubarb wine.'

This anecdote, although interesting in itself, didn't at the moment command much of the Applebys' attention. They were naturally anxious to determine the extent of the impropriety committed by their aged retainer.

'Just how did the trouble begin?' Appleby asked.

'Let me see.' Dr Dunton appeared to consider this question carefully. 'It must be said to have begun, I suppose, when I had this unfortunate thought of inviting Mrs Povey to open the sale. At the time, it seemed quite the right thing. She'd actually brought her husband to church one Sunday. Didn't stay for communion, but listened to the sermon most attentively. It was the one about the loaves and fishes, Lady Appleby. I dare say you remember it.'

'Yes, indeed. It's one of your best.' Judith Appleby was quite firm about this. 'But do you mean that Mr Povey of Brockholes has turned out to be married, after all? Everybody understood him to be a bachelor, didn't they?'

'Perfectly true—and so he was. His marriage has taken place—in a registry office, I fear—subsequently to his coming into residence among us. Quite a romantic and whirlwind affair. One understands that the lady, a Miss Porter, was professionally engaged at Brockholes, having received a commission to embellish and decorate the interior of the mansion. My new parishioner fell in love with her. And they were married—to express it vulgarly—at the drop of a handkerchief.'

'Fishy business,' Colonel Birch-Blackie commented. 'Queer lot, those Poveys. Always were. Not our sort. And some deuced odd goings-on at Brockholes at this moment, if you ask me. A lot of talk among the village folk. No smoke without fire, you know.'

'Ambrose has never quite forgotten his cigarette-box,' Mrs Birch-Blackie said indulgently. 'Just as our humbler neighbours seem never to have forgotten their wives and daughters.'

'Surely the poet Gray was sadly mistaken when he wrote of the short and simple annals of the poor.' Dr Dunton was delighted to have thought of this. 'The genealogies of Boxer's Bottom or of King's Yatter alone, I sometimes reflect, must surpass in complexity those of the Borgias themselves. And the oddest breaches of the tables of consanguinity, if seldom openly referred to, are equally seldom forgotten. I have read of primitive peoples whose entire lore consists of an exact knowledge of such matters within the tribe over a period of many generations. It is scarcely otherwise under our own greenwood tree.'

'But I take it,' Appleby said, 'that what you have called the provocation offered by Mrs Corp turned upon something altogether simpler?'

'Yes, indeed. I own to a certain admiration for Mrs Corp. She may be said openly to have proclaimed her shame (although, of course, everybody knew about it anyway) in the interest of securing some material advantage for her son Sammy, who is a young man not very well able to wrestle for the world's prizes himself.'

'Half-wit, eh?' Colonel Birch-Blackie said. 'Nice to see one or two still around, I always think. Mad-doctors far too keen on rounding them up and bunging them into their bins. Useless burden on the rates and so on, and only makes the poor devils miserable. Much better left pottering round the village pond, even if they go exposing themselves to old women, and all the rest of it.'

'There is much to be said, Colonel, for that robust and liberal point of view.' Dr Dunton had nodded approvingly. 'But let me return to Mrs Corp. Whether or not Mr Povey has actually acknowledged the paternity of her child, I do not know. But he has given her money, which was conceivably generous but undeniably injudicious.'

'And rather odd,' Appleby said.

'I agree, and the point is one to which I shall return in a moment. But here is Mrs Corp, one of a number of persons in our neighbourhood who prove to have tenacious and unfavourable memories of the new owner of Brockholes. It is rumoured that she marched Sammy up to the house—'

'It's not a rumour. It's a fact. I saw it happen.' Judith Appleby announced this calmly, but observed the Vicar to be somewhat taken aback. 'I was walking in the park, you see—and within view of the front door.'

'That is a most interesting circumstance. Mrs Corp, it seems, was rebuffed by some member of the household, and her next step was to make a great deal of fuss in the village.

Mr Povey was Sammy's father, and she was going to have the law on him. That sort of thing. I must not, out of any tenderness for Mrs Corp—in many ways so admirable a woman—mask the fact that she is of a somewhat intemperate habit. One may suspect that the vials of her wrath had been replenished with ale. Having thus largely advertised what she claimed to have been her former relationship with the new arrival at Brockholes, she returned there—no doubt again accompanied by Sammy—a few lays later. This time she encountered Charles Povey himself. On just what happened there is only her own word. Unless, of course, Lady Appleby—'

'I'm afraid not,' Judith said. 'Once was enough.'

'Quite so. Well, Mrs Corp's tale is to the effect that Povey listened to her for a time, evinced increasing signs of guilt and perturbation, and then suddeny produced a small fistful of ten-pound notes, thrust them at her, and walked rapidly away.'

'Ten-pound notes!' Mrs Birch-Blackie exclaimed. 'The man must be off his head.'

'Or demoralized,' Appleby said. 'And more probably that. I begin to suspect that in quite a variety of ways this mysterious millionaire is having rather a bad time. Did he accompany his bride when she opened your bazaar, Vicar?'

'Yes, he did—and he reminded me rather of a fellow let out of prison on parole. I've had to do with such characters in my time.'

'So Brockholes may be a kind of prison? A most suggestive idea.' Appleby was amused. 'And did Povey appear to enjoy his trip outside?'

'I don't suppose he enjoyed the little scene I now go on to describe, my dear Sir John. It would not have happened were not Mrs Corp a woman of some imagination. On what had she spent that money? I invite you to guess.'

'On dressing herself up.'

'Not at all. But on dressing Sammy up. She had dressed Sammy as a gentleman. And very skilfully, oddly enough. She must be a woman of sharp observation and considerable taste. The clothes were even right for the occasion. Sammy looked much as Lord Linger's elder boy would have looked, had he dreamed of turning out to our affair. Unfortunately it went down very badly.'

'With Povey and his wife?'

'No, no—with the rustic world at large. Everybody was outraged and furious.'

'How frightfully mean!' Judith Appleby was indignant. 'Why ever should they be?'

'It was felt to be a kind of jumping the gun on Mrs Corp's part. The more simple-minded probably believed that Sammy's new habiliments signified his actually having been adopted within the ranks of the gentry. Of having slipped from the wrong to the right side of the blanket, as it were, and being now virtually the heir of Brockholes. Your worthy Hoobin was among those who felt a sense of personal injustice before the spectacle. Why Sammy Corp, when there were so many equally valid claimants in every village around? And pre-eminent among these—Mr Hoobin loudly averred—his own nephew Solo. He hauled Solo forward, and bade the company at large to remark his Povey nose. Fortunately I was supported that afternoon by both my sons, it being the last week of the Oxford vacation. They hustled the Hoobins into the vicarage, plied them with cider until they were stupefied, and then drove them home. I can only hope that they were fit for their work here next day.'

'And then all went well?' Judith asked.

'All went smoothly for the remainder of the sale. The Poveys walked round, buying this and that in the manner expected of them.'

'With ten-pound notes?'

'Well, yes. But one may suppose such currency to con-

stitute a tycoon's notion of small change. Mrs Povey—when
she had recovered from the Hoobins's unfortunate demons-
tration—appeared greatly to enjoy the whole affair. Perhaps
she had never previously had an opportunity of playing lady
of the manor. She was handed a bouquet by one of the
Heyhoe children in a pink frock. There appear to be about
a hundred of them in the parish. Heyhoe children, that is;
not pink frocks. Mrs Povey received the tribute most grace-
fully. She might positively have been a royal, Lady
Appleby, doing her thing, as the young peeople say, on a
more august occasion of the same sort. My own reflection
was that the poor lady must be leading rather a boring life
at Brockholes so avidly to have seized upon our small junket-
ing as a vehicle of *divertissement*. Indeed, the whole spectacle of Brockholes troubles me, I am bound to admit. That
grotesque fence, for example. One supposes such things to
have been erected round concentration camps.'

'Is it to keep people in?' Mrs Birch-Blackie asked. 'Or to
keep people out?'

'Primarily,' Appleby said, 'I see it as neither. It is essentially an exercise in public relations.'

This enigmatic comment produced a moment's silence at
Lady Appleby's luncheon table.

'Public relations?' Colonel Birch-Blackie then reiterated
blankly. 'Explain yourself, my dear fellow. Looks more like
private relations to me.'

'Very well. This man Charles Povey has a reputation as a
financier—or whatever it's to be called—eccentrically given
to a reclusive and elusive way of life. The fence is designed
to play up on that idea. Povey, for reasons unknown to us,
judges himself—or is judged by advisers—to be at risk when
he walks at large. All sorts of explanations are possible. I'm
only surprised, Vicar, that he turned out even for your small
but laudable occasion.'

'Quite so. I take the point.' Dr Dunton was unoffended by this placing of his annual jamboree. 'I'm sometimes surprised that I face up to it myself.' The Vicar chuckled comfortably over this unprofessional avowal. 'Parish fêtes can pretty well be fates worse than death, eh?'

Mrs Birch-Blackie was amused by this joke. To her husband, however, it had to be explained; and this held up the discussion for a moment. Appleby then continued his speculative course.

'They're after him, if you ask me. Gunning for him—as, my dear Vicar, your young people say. Who "they" can be, I don't know at all. But the chap himself gets restless, even desperate. Part of him is screaming to be let out. Perhaps his newly acquired wife is screaming too. And they make a little break for it to your admirable sale. Quite a mystery, the whole affair.'

'A mystery?' Colonel Birch-Blackie had a flair for coming in on an interrogative note. He hesitated. 'Oughtn't to repeat the gossip of a club,' he continued gruffly. 'Still, I have heard something rather odd. Happened when I last ran up to town. Fellow in the City heard I was this chap's neighbour, and murmured a thing or two. The Povey concerns are in a damnable mess, it seems. Scores of people will presently be calling themselves creditors. Anxious Povey won't bolt from the country, and so on. Shocking state of affairs. Said even to have set spies on him. Disgraceful situation. Man's a considerable land-owner, after all.'

'That would explain my Ent,' Judith Appleby said.

Not unnaturally, it was only Appleby who failed to find this an obscure remark. Mrs Birch-Blackie, however, had been pursuing a thought of her own, and she now came out with it.

'Charles Povey ought never to have come back to Brockholes. It wasn't even his property. He had to buy it. And he was simply running his neck into a noose.'

'Corps and Hoobins?' Appleby asked. 'Only a petty sort of noose, that. It can't really be what's now controlling the man's way of life.'

'Probably not. But it needn't be vast financial troubles either. He shuts himself away because morbidly sensitive.'

'Morbidly sensitive?' Colonel Birch-Blackie repeated. 'Extraordinary things you sometimes say, Jane. Often can't make head or tail of them. No getting a handle on them. Comes of reading all those rubbishing novels from the County Library. By papists and communists and unnatural women. Litter the place. Can't think why you do it. Damn it, woman, you can still sit a horse.'

Mrs Birch-Blackie was quite unperturbed at being thus publicly indicted of a premature indulgence in literary pursuits. She simply turned to Appleby and continued her remarks.

'My uncle Gerald, for example,' she said. 'He had only one ear. There was really nothing out of the way about it. He could hear perfectly well. It was simply a congenital thing, which happens to turn up in my family a couple of times in a century or thereabout. Distinguished in a way—like haemophilia, and oddities of that sort. But my uncle was always extremely touchy about it. You might have expected it to wear off as he grew older. Not a bit of it. He eventually resigned his perfectly safe seat in parliament. In his last years, if he simply couldn't avoid going out to dinner, he wore a black silk balaclava helmet. People used to suppose he was a Tibetan lama, or something of that sort.'

'A reasonable misapprehension.' Appleby was impressed. 'And has Charles Povey only one ear to?'

'All that Mr Povey lacks is the index-finger of his left hand. But he may be extremely sensitive about that.'

'I see.' Appleby sounded unconvinced. 'Another matter of congenital malformation?'

'Nothing of the kind. Merely an accident when he was a young man. But there was an ugly rumour about it at the time—and, of course, that might induce morbid feelings in him later. It was said that the finger had been chopped off by his brother Arthur.'

'It sounds a most revolting accident.'

'No, not an accident. An entirely deliberate action. And in a wood-shed, they say, which makes it appear particularly squalid.'

There was a moment's silence. Appleby appeared not much concerned with the logic of Mrs Birch-Blackie's last remark. Rather, he might have been gazing into hiding-places many years deep.

'Arthur?' he said. 'A younger brother—and haven't I heard he lost his life at sea?'

'You probably have. It was in the papers at the time. Charles and Arthur were on a yacht together. And something fell on Arthur and brained him.'

'And Charles suffered various privations thereafter?'

'Apparently. Yes—there was a bit about that too.'

'A harrowing incident, no doubt. It might itself affect Charles Povey's temperament, don't you think? Turn him into a bit of a recluse, and so forth.'

'No occasion for treating yourself to a ten-foot fence,' Colonel Birch-Blackie said. 'But one sympathises, of course. Bad show, losing a brother. Even if he did once take a chopper to you.'

'Perfectly true.' Appleby concurred with these sage observations as if from a certain absence of mind. Indeed, his interest in Mr Charles Povey of Brockholes Abbey seemed to have evaporated. 'Coffee in the library, I think,' he said. 'I rather want your advice, Birch-Blackie, on a bit of drainage we're thinking of in the field beyond the spinney.'

'My dear fellow, I'll be delighted.'

'Good. I'll be most grateful.' Appleby got to his feet. 'We feel it's quite important,' he said. 'We're thinking about it a lot.'

The subject thus proposed for conference proved to open up a somewhat wider field of discussion than Appleby had perhaps reckoned. Colonel Birch-Blackie had heard favourable reports of a new type of land drain, approximately twice the normal length, particularly designed for use where there was likely to be trouble from moles. And Dr Dunton proved to have relevant facts fresh in mind, since he had been conducting a spirited dispute with higher ecclesiastical authorities on the troublesome frequency with which floodwater made its way into his glebe. It was a further hour, therefore, before the guests took their departure. Appleby saw the Birch-Blackies punctiliously into their car. He walked with the Vicar (who wheeled his bicycle) to the bottom of the Long Dream drive. Then he returned to the house at a very brisk pace indeed. He was glancing at his watch as he crossed the hall—so that Judith, who was helping Mrs Colpoys to clear up, glanced at him curiously, but said noththing. He went into the butler's pantry, which nowadays accommodated not a manservant but a deep-freeze and a telephone. It was the telephone to which he turned.

'Please get me,' he said briskly to the operator, 'the General Infirmary in Adelaide, South Australia.'

XII

Until rather late that night Appleby continued to speculate sometimes through the medium of remarks thrown out to Judith, sometimes broodingly inside his own head.

'Buzfuz,' he said. 'That's what this antipodean sawbones insisted on calling the brothers. Medical etiquette and so forth. Protecting a patient's privacy and confidence. Fair enough, I suppose. But if he'd been prepared to call a Povey a Povey I'd have known where we are long ago. Or approximately where we are. For it's an uncommon puzzle still.'

'Did he mind being routed out?'

'The good Professor Budgery? He wasn't too cordial at first. It was at an unconscionable hour, I suppose. The huntsmen up in America, and chaps already past their first sleep in Persia. But he was perfectly forthcoming when I'd explained a bit. His Colin and Adam Buzfuz *were* Charles and Arthur Povey. And the craft he called the *Jabberwock* was really the *Gay Phoenix*. Equally silly names for a boat, if you ask me.'

'Did Budgery tell you anything new?'

'No, not really. But then I had a go—another confoundedly expensive telephone call—at the Chief Justice of the place.'

'Delusions of grandeur, I call that. And surely there wasn't a law-case about the affair?'

'No, no—it was just that this old chap was at that dinner I told you about. It came back to me that he'd hinted a wholesome scepticism in the face of the whole yarn—the whole medical history, or whatever it's to be called. As we drove down to Adelaide together he even murmured to me something to the effect that he suspected a bit of monkey-business about the affair. Well, so did I, in a dim enough way. So I wanted to check whether he'd had in mind what had vaguely hovered in my own thick skull. He had.'

'Which was what?'

'Well, now, that's hard to say.'

'Don't be idiotic, John. If you suspected something, and this old judge-person suspected the same thing, you must *know* what it was, or is, that you both suspected, or suspect.'

'Most precisely expressed. But just what do *you* think the horrid thought is?'

'What happened on the *Gay Phoenix* wasn't an accident.'

'Just what do you mean by that?'

'I mean that Arthur Povey, the younger brother, didn't die as a result of something falling on him.'

'Ah! Looked at strictly, you know, that's a somewhat ambiguous constatation.'

'Don't be pedantic.'

'All right. Let's take the thing quite simply. The story begins, in the solitude of the Pacific Ocean, on straight Cain-and-Abel lines. An elder brother kills a younger. It's perfectly conceivable. Fratricide happens to be not all that common in the modern world, but it does sometimes happen. And here we have a history of something like bad blood between the brothers—although the evidence for it lies only in that wood-shed a long time ago.'

'And the story may merely have been malicious gossip. That's never in short supply in these parts.'

'Too true. But if there really was a smouldering antagonism between Charles and Arthur Povey it's reasonable to maintain that weeks at sea with only one another's company might well produce a flare-up. But it's all completely speculative, is it not? So now consider another thing. There were these two men alone together in an inviolable privacy—and on a yacht which probably bore, and would retain, the signs of having taken a terrific pounding from storms in which any disaster might occur. It's hard to imagine more ideal conditions for the undetectable murder. If Charles Povey killed Arthur Povey in that way he had, and has, absolutely nothing to worry about.'

'Except a trifle on his conscience.'

'Quite so. His crime might well drive him insane, or the next thing to it. It might induce all sorts of bizarre behaviour. It might render him a very dangerous man indeed, prone to further violent acts without rational motivation of any sort. All that's obvious. But my point is this: at the level of cold reason this murderer has no worries at all—so it's no use trying to explain any conduct subsequently observed in him as logically adopted under some compulsion arising from his deed. I'll give you an example. If one were writing a yarn about the thing one might call it *The Case of the Elusive Tycoon*. It seems that Charles Povey has played something like that role for quite a long time—but now he has grotesquely stepped it up. The fellow calling himself Bread—about whom a certain amount of thinking may usefully be done—plugged the idea, you remember, when I had my odd encounter with him. For blameless and indeed edifying reasons, Mr Charles Povey of Brockholes Abbey is more and more withdrawing from the observation of the world. We have to ask ourselves why. It's not because he's a murderer—for the simple reason that, as we agree, he's utterly safe on that front already.

'It's because his business interests are in a very bad way—and even perhaps in danger of being exposed as largely fraudulent. He's in danger of being bankrupted and even exposed as a crook, so he's lying low.'

There was a silence during which Appleby stuffed a pipe and lit it. Judith, who had been messing about with some

164

clay on a board in front of her, continued this activity with increased concentration. An observer might have concluded that they had tacitly agreed to drop the Brockholes mystery as boring. But then suddenly Appleby spoke again.

'That won't do either,' he said. 'Up to a point, the remote control mythos can no doubt be useful to a shady operator. But when there's real pressure on him—when his financial probity and viability are being radically questioned, and so on—it can't be in his interest to carry the turn to a bizarre extreme. It leads to private enquiry agents hiding themselves in hides, and heaven knows what. No! The man must have some other reason to fear the common traffic of life—whether on the business front, or the social front, or both. So he's taking all the subsidiary risks that attend making himself appear very eccentric indeed. Or somebody is compelling him to play it that way. Bread, perhaps. Or this new Mrs Povey. Or—again—both.'

'There's all this business of bastards and so on.'

'Poppycock! It has no doubt been disconcerting to find the district still a petty hornets' nest in that way.' Appleby had let his pipe go out. He put it down on the table beside him. 'Of course,' he said slowly, 'he may find that he has some quite different, and vastly larger, danger to fear from the persistence of rustic memories. Returning to Brockholes may have been a disastrous miscalculation. He has exposed himself to hazard on two fronts instead of one.' Appleby paused. 'And why the devil should he get married?' he added.

'Why ever should he not?' Judith Appleby was mildly amused. 'Men do. They fall suddenly in love. And if they're virtuous, or the lady is, marriage follows—and often with all convenient speed.'

'I have a sense of it as out of character in this particular case, all the same. He's got along quite happily without marriage through the better part of a lifetime. Why muck in now?'

'Nothing in the world is more common than the marriage of hardened bachelors in middle age. You're a case in point, darling.'

'Damn it, woman, I was twenty-nine!' Appleby, comically outraged, had sat bolt upright. 'This is a perfectly idiotic conversation,' he said severely.

'It's nothing of the sort. You're moving in on something. Remorselessly—like one of those bloodhounds in old-fashioned thrillers. I recognize the signs.'

'The whole affair is no business of mine.'

'And I've heard *that* quite recently.' To an effect of muted drama, Judith thrust a scalpel into the heart of the little maquette on which she had been working. 'So what happens now?' she asked.

'What happens,' Appleby said, 'is that we go to bed. And I'll drop in on Brockholes again tomorrow. Undeniably, it's an interesting place.'

But something happened before that. It was in the small hours that Appleby, totally against his habit, found himself suddenly wide awake. He sat up in bed, and then—equally unwontedly—called out urgently to his wife.

'Judith, wake up!'

'John, what on earth is it? Burglars—a fire?' Judith had flicked on a light and was sitting up too.

'Nothing of the kind. But listen. You remember my saying that something you said was an ambiguous constatation?'

'For pity's sake! I don't know what you're talking about. Tell me at breakfast. Go to sleep.'

'Wait a minute. You really must listen. I really don't think I quite knew what I meant. But I do now. You had said that perhaps Arthur Povey didn't die as a result of something falling on him. What you meant was that his brother

Charles murdered him. Isn't that right? But your words could have meant something else. *Arthur* Povey didn't die as a result of something falling on him. It was *Charles* Povey who died that way.'

'John, you've been dreaming. You've been having a nightmare. You probably drank too much before coming to bed.'

'Nothing of the sort. It's simply that the truth of this affair has jumped at me. All that business about the storm-tossed Povey in hospital, for a start. It didn't ring true. The Chief Justice thought it didn't. I thought it didn't.'

'You've gone off your head, John dear. Do you really think that Budgery, a perfectly responsible professor of medicine, was spinning you and his other guests a pack of lies?'

'Of course not. He was simply taken in. He and his assistants in that hospital were simply taken in—and by an uncommonly cunning rascal. It was the younger Povey, Arthur, who survived in the *Gay Phoenix*—only he claimed to be his wealthy elder brother, Charles. But I'm wrong. He did better than that. He allowed himself, but most reluctantly, to be *persuaded* he was Charles. He had those doctors sweating blood to cure him of the weird psychological aberration —as they conceived it to be—that he wasn't himself but his brother.' Appleby was suddenly as excited as a boy. 'No imposture can have had a more brilliant flying start in all recorded history!'

'I see. And now we can go to sleep.'

'Judith, don't be maddening. Can't you see how it all fits? What we're looking for is a rational explanation of this man's returning unwarily to Brockholes—and equally of his going so madly reclusive there. He came because he had very little notion of his brother Charles's final reputation as an amorist and general bad hat. And he's gone to earth and put up this story of retiring from the world and its sordid concerns simply because he has found that on no other terms can the imposture or impersonation or whatever it's to be called be sustained. I shouldn't be surprised if that ex-crook Bread knows the truth about him, and has him under his thumb as a result. And his bride the former Miss Porter too, for that matter.'

'And John Appleby. Well, well!'

'Yes—and John Appleby. But I'm blessed if I know what the retired copper is going to do about it.'

'I thought you were going over to Brockholes first thing in the morning.'

'I have my doubts about it now. What does it matter who calls himself Charles Povey? Whoever he is, he looks like being booked for a packet of trouble without my shoving in.'

'It's no good, John. Of course you'll have to go. It wouldn't be you if you didn't. Just sleep on that.'

'I suppose you're right. I know you're right. Sorry to have disturbed you. Good night again.'

'Good morning,' Judith said. And she turned over and went to sleep.

XIII

I T M I G H T B E better—Appleby told himself as he drove off next morning—to take this whole dubious business to the police. However fantastic the story seemed, the local constabulary would certainly listen to him with quite oppressive respect. Or he could take it straight to the Chief Constable, who was an old friend, with a stiff off-the-record injunction that he himself was not to be further involved in any way. That would be what might be called the dignified thing to do. It wasn't in the least dignified to do any more private poking round himself; if he did, he might very soon find himself feeling rather like Judith's bird-watching acquaintance in his hide. And if his own bird-watching resulted in his turning up, so to speak, a mare's nest he would feel a thorough fool if a word of it got around. Moreover, he remembered gloomily, he had never, when a policeman himself, much managed to like busybody citizens who presented themselves with implausible stories of dirty work at the cross-roads. This had been very wrong of him—for hadn't it been part of his job constantly to urge upon the public their bounden duty to call a copper the moment they smelt a rat or even a mouse?

Appleby found himself scowling over the bonnet of his antique Rover as he drove. This welter of bad metaphors—rats at the cross-roads—seemed to mirror a most discreditable confusion of mind. He was even in a kind of philosophical muddle. Supposing it to be true that this fellow call-himself Charles Povey *was* really Arthur Povey, just what did the fact signify to a reasonable man? Charles had got himself blipped on the head by a mast, and Arthur had nipped in and taken, as it were, the vacant family niche. There seemed every indication that, morally speaking, the brothers had been much of a muchness—each, you might say, a shade more than average-worthless human beings. So what? Arthur, on the whole, sounded a slightly less unappealing character than his brother. He had at least—granting the truth of the story—embarked on a project of impressively breath-taking audacity. So what were people for? It came down to that. Bobby Appleby—youngest of the Applebys and a most advanced novelist—would at this point offer, if applied to, remarks on a senseless universe; would back up the enterprising Arthur on existentialist principles—adding, as he went along, sage reflections on all property as theft. Bobby, on the other hand, would unobtrusively drop from the circle of his acquaintance anybody who had formed the habit of acquiring his reading-matter from the bookshops in a slightly irregular way. There were areas in which one had to keep theory and practice distinct. But what would Bobby do if he happened to detect a total stranger helping himself to novels or biographies or treatises on pastoral theology from the shelves of Messrs Hatchards or Sir Basil Blackwell? Would he call a copper at once? Appleby found he hadn't a clue. It was depressing that the minds of the young should be so opaque to one.

But what if that mast *hadn't* fallen on the true Charles? What if, as Judith had conjectured, Arthur had murdered his brother? It was remarkable how much—short of a position of complete nihilism—this altered the picture. (Or equally, Appleby added to himself carefully, if Charles had murdered Arthur—the straight Cain-and-Abel thing.) But this was precisely what nobody was ever going to know. Or not short of complete confession on the murderer's part.

Appleby had been dawdling along the road. The Rover had been nearing Brockholes too rapidly for his liking, since muddle was a poor companion to take with one on such an assignment as he was visualizing. But now he stepped on the accelerator. It had become perfectly clear that his business was to discover the truth. Not merely about who lived in the house ahead of him. He couldn't believe that would be very difficult. But about what had really happened in the middle of the Pacific Ocean. And that might be very difficult indeed. In fact, his sort of thing.

We are not now that strength which in old days
Moved earth and heaven . . .

Appleby, slowing before a bend, chanted the words of Ulysses in innocent hyperbole.

. . . that which we are, we are . . .

He braked violently, and swerved to the side of the road. It had been a very near shave. Indeed, there had been quite a bump.

The car confronting him, which had been travelling at a shocking pace, was a Rolls-Royce. Its number-plate read *CP* I. Appleby (probably like most private gentlemen) thought the number-plate game a badge of vulgar ostentation. Still, it was perhaps useful to be thus instantly apprised that here was a vehicle almost certainly in the proprietorship of Mr Charles Povey (or his supplanter). There were two occupants—or there had been, since one of them, the driver, had now climbed out on the road and was advancing upon Appleby without cordiality. Neither car had escaped damage. The Rover, which might be regarded as representing a middling station in life, had reasonably held its own in this confrontation with automotive aristocracy. It showed a slightly dented front wing. But the Rolls did too.

The approaching driver, although the blame had been entirely his, was plainly preparing to adopt a stance of high indignation. Was he perhaps Povey (Charles or Arthur) himself? Appleby instantly saw that he was not. Confronting him was the bearded secretary, Bread by name but cake by nature, whose almost certainly criminal past Appleby again found himself tiresomely unable to pin-point. But if Appleby didn't know quite all about Bread, Bread certainly knew all about Appleby. He had been about to provoke a flaming row (since that is the routine resource of aggressive and culpable motorists) when he realized in whose company he had landed himself. His jaw dropped, and Appleby had a sharp immediate impression of obscure panic as having gripped the man.

'Good heavens!' Bread said with a rather weak air of astonishment. 'Sir John Appleby, isn't it? I remember that nice chat we had. Sorry about this. My fault, I'm sure. But there's no real damage done. Settle up later, eh? Let the insurance fellows work it out. Just drive on.'

'Not quite immediately, Mr Bread.' Appleby got out of the Rover and glanced at the position of the Rolls. It was well on his own side of the road, since Bread had been dangerously cutting a corner. Even so, each car was blocking the path of the other; neither could proceed on its way even after reversing until the other shifted its position too. 'One must act regularly in these cases,' Appleby went on heavily. 'There's always the possibility of personal injury, you know. Or delayed shock. To yourself, for example, or to your passenger. The lady may be upset.'

'Nothing of the kind. Nothing of the kind, I assure you. She said so, just as I nipped out. "I'm right as rain," she said. "We'll just drive on." Have to catch a train, as a matter of fact. So I'll be obliged, Sir John, if you'll back clear and let me pass.' Bread, as he said this, wasn't quite in control of his manner or his voice; it was just as if he'd restrained himself from employing some such variant as 'if you'll bloody well piss off'.

Appleby took licence from this to produce the offended

frown and freezing courtesy of a person of consequence in the community.

'I'm so sorry,' he said, 'but I really think not. I'm afraid I must ask you to do the correct thing, sir. We wait until another car comes along, and we ask the driver to notify the police. They'll then be here in no time.'

For a moment Bread said nothing. He eyed Appleby narrowly, with a gaze both baffled and alarmed. He must have concluded that Appleby's *ad hoc* conception of the correct thing was something he wasn't going to be argued out of.

'Oh, very well,' he said. 'As you please. But it's extremely inconvenient.'

'In that case I must hasten to apologize to your passenger. I take it she is Mrs Povey?'

'Yes, she is.' Bread had hesitated over this reply; he was clearly a fellow whose second nature was prevarication. 'But I'll just move the Rolls back a little first.'

'Better not, I think. The exact position of the two vehicles is important, you know.' Bread, Appleby had decided, was in so alarmed a state that he was quite capable of reversing the Rolls rapidly into distance. 'And I must certainly introduce myself at once. It's the civil thing, considering that we are virtually neighbours.'

This comedy of punctilio took Appleby to the open door of the Rolls. Mrs Povey, who had been in front with Bread, hadn't moved from her seat. It wouldn't have been easy to do so, since the rest of the car's interior was crammed with expensive-looking luggage. She was a striking woman, by no means very quietly dressed, and she was calming her nerves with a cigarette.

'Mrs Povey?' he said. 'I'm so sorry about this. My name is Appleby, and I live in the neighbourhood. If I haven't yet had the pleasure of making myself known to your husband it's only because I've been abroad for some months. My wife is much looking forward to meeting you. Mr Bread I do know, since I met him just before going away. We had a most interesting talk. As a matter of fact, I had a curious sense of having come across him in different circumstances in the past. Without a beard, I am inclined to think. But the precise occasion eludes me.'

If Mrs Povey, formerly Miss Porter, was perturbed by this speech (as she well might have been by such unnecessarily communicative remarks) she contrived not to reveal the fact.

'How do you do?' she said. 'How very nice. I do adore meeting famous people. But I am very anxious to catch my train.'

'Is Mr Bread going to catch it too?'

This question—undeniably irregular from a strictly social point of view—did produce an effect. Mrs Povey jumpily stubbed out her cigarette in the thing that Rolls-Royces provide for the purpose.

'Mr Bread,' she said nervously, and with seemingly meaningless evasiveness, 'is my husband's secretary. But perhaps you know that.'

'Quite so. I'm sure he is invaluable. But I hope nothing serious has happened?'

'Serious? Of course not. I don't see why—'

'Your car, if I may say so, *was* travelling rather fast. And your train seems so important. There hasn't been any sort of crisis at Brockholes? I'd be most anxious to help.'

Mrs Povey was not now standing up very well to this war of nerves—which Appleby had to acknowledge as one of his more oddly intuitive performances. It had its origin, no doubt, in a prompting to subject the lady's husband, when he could get hold of him, to something of the same sort.

'My mother,' Mrs Povey said, 'has met with a serious accident in London. I am hastening to her.'

'But I understood you to say that nothing serious had happened?' Appleby, who might have been the most obtuse

of men, glanced behind Mrs Povey. 'I am extremely sorry
to hear such bad news, but it's comforting you had time to
pack. Perhaps, in the circumstances, we had better not wait
for the police after all.'

'No, please don't let us do that.' Mrs Povey's eagerness
was sudden and extreme. It came to Appleby, quite simply,
that she was a woman in flight. She wasn't hastening anywhere; she was merely bolting from Brockholes—fleeing, it
might be said, the connubial dwelling. And it looked as if
Bread had a similar aim in view. He was quite as anxious
to make himself scarce as his employer's wife was, and he
now contributed to the conversation on a changed and con-
ciliatory note. It was, indeed, an ingratiating note, such as
Appleby could dimly remember as once familiar to him
among persons holding some acquaintance with Her
Majesty's prisons.

'That's most considerate of you, Sir John,' Bread said.
'We're really very anxious—very anxious, indeed. Such a
nice lady, dear old Mrs Porter. You've probably met her,
seeing she's prominent in Society. And so sudden an illness!
Mrs Povey is naturally in great anxiety. One of those
treacherous cerebral things. We're here today and gone tomorrow, Sir John. Like the flowers of the forest. *Eheu
fugaces*, as the poet says.'

These reflections—mildly surprising if one was un-
acquainted with Bread (or Butter) the reading man—
appeared to call for no reply. Appleby murmured some civil
farewell to the distressed Mrs Povey, and turned away towards his car. Then a thought seemed to strike him.

'Is Mr Povey at home?' he asked. 'He must be most
anxious, too. I wonder if he'd care for a call from a new
neighbour? It might serve to divert his thoughts, don't you
think?'

Mrs Povey and Mr Bread observably exchanged a swift
and apprehensive glance. Conceivably it wasn't obscure to

either of them that this pestilent former Police Commissioner would now make his way to Brockholes whether they liked it or not.

'But of course!' Mrs Povey said with random and misplaced effusiveness. She had undeniably become a thoroughly frightened woman, so that Appleby found himself wondering what on earth could really have happened. 'Do call, Sir John. Arthur will be quite delighted.'

This staggering instance of what the learned term the psycho-pathology of everyday life didn't cause a flicker on Appleby's now almost vacuously polite face, and the perturbed lady herself appeared quite unconscious of what she had inadvertently revealed. (Or *was* it inadvertent? The inner Appleby, long habituated to thinking twice about anything he heard within a context of suspected crime, asked himself this automatically. Wheels within wheels, perhaps? One simply never knew.) Appleby's glance had gone instantly to Bread, and he had to tell himself that Bread was by no means inconsiderable. Bread's expression hadn't flickered either, although he couldn't have failed to register what on any simple calculation had been a potentially disastrous slip.

'Then I'll certainly drop in.' Appleby smiled benignly, produced the sort of bow that the cerebrally stricken Mrs Porter (being habituated to the most refined social circles) would have approved at once, and returned to his own car.

It all remained, he reflected, as speculative as you please. But there was much to be said for the view that this precious couple were throwing the poor devil to the wolves. And he still wasn't sure that it was a wolf he himself wanted to be.

As if in the kind of dream that goes in for reduplicated disasters, the late near-accident all but repeated itself only a few hundred yards ahead. This time, what hurtled round a bend and saved itself only with a swerve and a scream of brakes was that sort of mini-bus or shooting-wagon in which members of the larger landed gentry are accustomed to truck around small *corvées* of men and youths impounded to beat up pheasants for the purposes of ritual slaughter. But the vehicle was not being thus used now. Its large roof-rack was crammed with suitcases and bundles, and with the exception of the driver the occupants were all females.

The driver, reduced to backing and then edging cautiously past, took a look at Appleby. Appleby took a look at the driver. As in the case of Bread some months before, a factor of recognition came instantaneously into play. This time, however, Appleby could put a name to the man as certainly as the man could put a name to Appleby. Nor was this all. The females, because accommodated facing inwards on benches running the length of the wagon, were not clearly distinguishable. Even so—if but for a brief moment— Appleby was aware of what might be termed old familiar faces : several of them. He had last viewed them, years before, as they stood in the dock at the Central Criminal Court before taking up a spell of residence in Holloway Goal.

They were gone—and clearly with all their worldly possessions swaying on the roof above them. It was evidence of a most precipitate and dramatic exodus from the Poveys' ancestral home.

XIV

BUT THERE WAS no difficulty in finding the proprietor of the mansion. He was standing before his front door, gazing bemusedly up and down the broad terrace upon which it gave, and apparently in the very act of realizing that he was the sole remaining inhabitant.

The rats had abandoned the sinking ship. Another flat and faded metaphor, Appleby told himself. Would it be apter to say that the little rats had abandoned the big rat? Big or little, there was nothing particularly rat-like about Mr Povey. He looked exhausted, harassed, even a thoroughly sick man. But he would have passed anywhere as a well-bred Englishman still in vigorous middle age; when not, as now, in some state of shock, he probably commanded that air of unobtrusive self-assurance and untroubled authority which marks the man of property. If indeed an impostor, he started off with certain natural advantages as a consequence of this. In fact, Appleby thought, when normally poised he might be quite a tough nut to crack. Which was all the more reason for sailing in at once. With this final mix-up of banal images, Appleby strode up a short flight of steps.

'Mr Povey?' he said. 'I must introduce myself. My name is Appleby.'

'Yes, of course, Sir John. I've heard of you as one of my new neighbours—and professionally as well, I need hardly say.' Mr Povey, although his awareness appeared to have focused itself with difficulty upon this sudden irruption of a fresh hazard in his environment, and although his quick smile was tight and carefully controlled, took a step forward and shook hands in proper form. 'Delighted to meet you. How do you do?'

This reception quite cheered Appleby up. It was in his nature to hate what might be termed a walk-over, and now he knew at once that nothing of the sort was on offer. He might end up with something abject on his hands, but meanwhile there was going to be a fight. The chap *was* tough: not a doubt of it. Or at least—Appleby added as an afterthought—he was quick-witted and resilient, which came to approximately the same thing.

'I've just met Mrs Povey,' Appleby said. 'Driving away.'

'Ah, yes. I suggested it.'

'And also—you'll forgive me—what looked like your entire domestic staff as well.'

'Their annual outing, that. Quite a good idea, really. And falls out conveniently, as it happens. Spare me a bit of gossip, and so on. The fact is, Sir John, I find myself with something of a crisis on my hands. A business crisis. Comes a fellow's way every now and then in my wretched walk of life.'

'Then I'm intruding, and must take myself off. I'm so sorry. We must meet again when you are more at leisure. I do apologize. Good-bye.'

'Nothing of the kind. Won't do at all.' Mr Povey had perceptibly squared his shoulders. 'That sort of thing mustn't interfere with the civilized social thing, eh? Do please come in.' And Mr Povey turned briskly and decisively towards the house.

'That's awfully kind.' Appleby—whom nothing would in fact have induced to quit Brockholes at the moment—lost no time in accepting this development. He followed his host into a large square hall. It was sheathed, not very appositely in view of the spuriously mediaeval exterior of the dwelling, in chilly white marble. They moved on from this into a library which, on the other hand, was of the most orthodox

and impressive country-house order. It was a good background for Mr Povey, were he proposing a last-ditch pro-
jection of himself as orthodox and impressive too.

'I suppose you've seen *The Times* today?' Povey asked.
He didn't make the mistake, Appleby noted, of speaking
with any sort of casual air.

'Not yet. I usually keep it till after lunch.'

'It has the whole bag of tricks—in a restrained way. Other
papers—I see none of them—will certainly be splashing the
thing.'

'The thing?'

'But won't you sit down, Sir John? And take a glass of
sherry?'

'Thank you.' Appleby sat down. 'But no sherry, thank
you very much. It's a shade early.'

'So it is.' Povey concurred in this sound judgement without fuss. 'As for the thing—well, it's hard to estimate its
dimensions at the moment. But I don't mind telling you
this. It wouldn't have surprised me in the least if you'd
turned out to be the Official Receiver.'

'Dear me! I'm extremely sorry to hear it.'

'Figuratively speaking, of course. I don't suppose he
potters about the countryside with a brief-case. Still, it looks
precious near to ruin. One must just face up to it.'

'Manfully.'

'Just that.' Mr Povey had given Appleby a sharp look.
'The truth is that I've been let down badly by a host of
subordinates. But I mustn't complain, Sir John. I have
nobody to blame but myself. Fact is, my mind has been more
and more on other things. I'd like you to see my pedigree
herd. Pictures, too. Latest accession is a rather nice
Caravaggio. But there won't be any more of that. No regrets,
however. I'm much occupied, to tell you the truth, with
philosophical and religious questions. Natural, you know, as
one grows older. I shall be wholly content if, at the end of

this shindy, the fellows who clear it up leave me the most modest competence. It's still perfectly possible to live quietly on ten thousand a year. Eight, if need be.'

'Or even seven.' Appleby contributed to this Dutch auction with entire gravity. 'And I'm most interested—most interested and edified, if I may venture to say so—to hear of your increasingly serious and elevated cast of mind. Would you ascribe the change to any particular circumstance in your life?'

'No, I hardly think so.' Appleby was conscious of receiving another sharp glance. 'Simply a matter of years bringing the philosophic habit along. It's mentioned by Wordsworth —always my favourite poet. I'm very fond of nature, and so forth.'

'Ah, yes. I was thinking, I suppose, of your brother's death in such tragic circumstances. Such an experience might well have a profound effect on a man. I forget your brother's name?'

'Arthur.' Mr Povey gave this information with perhaps a shade of unnecessary emphasis. He paused, and then added, firmly and quietly : 'I'm absolutely clear as to that.'

These were surprising words. Pondered, they even became bewildering. If the man who had uttered them was indeed Charles Povey, they were of course literally true. But their truth was of an order which no sane man could feel prompted to enunciate. Nobody can be other than clear about a brother's Christian name, whether that brother be dead or alive. If, on the other hand, the man now present in this library was Arthur Povey, he had backed up his lie in a singularly inept fashion.

Confronted with these facts, Appleby felt what he acknowledged to be a rather childish relief. It *wasn't* a mare's nest, and in pushing around Brockholes in a suspicious way he at least couldn't be charged with making a simple ass of himself.

A few minutes ago, the only irreducible fact had been that the financial affairs connected with the name of Charles Povey were in a singularly bad way; that a surprising number of persons had absented themselves abruptly from Brock-holes as a consequence; and that one of these, Povey's wife, had produced what was at the very least a surprising slip of the tongue. It was now certain that there existed an authentic mystery beyond all this; and that the mystery ultimately turned on a problem of identity precisely as he had supposed it must. That this clarification of the affair had been brought about by six words deliberately uttered by a man to all appearances fully in control of himself was a fact that required pondering. Meanwhile, however, something had to be said.

'Arthur, of course,' Appleby murmured blandly. 'My wife, by the way, remembers both of you. She was a Raven, you know.'

'Yes, of course. I look forward to meeting her when all this is over, Sir John. A notable family in these parts.'

'Quite so. You no doubt recall something of Judith's uncles, Everard and Luke. What was notable about them was a vein of very considerable eccentricity, after all.'

'Yes. That's to say, I may have heard so.' Povey paused. 'By Jove, yes! Wasn't there a famous business of lighting a beacon-fire on the church tower at Dream?'

'There was, indeed. But that was long before my time. You must have been no more than a boy.'

'Perfectly true.' Mr Povey had the air of a man prepared, even in a crisis of his affairs, to indulge a casual visitor in garrulous reminiscences.

'But that's all water under the bridge, wouldn't you say? I think we must have a few common acquaintances of much more recent date.'

'Possibly so.' Just perceptibly, Mr Povey tautened himself on his chair.

'Professor Budgery, for example.'

'Budgery?'

'The doctor who attended you in Australia after your terrible experience.'

'Yes, indeed. Efficient chap. I was most grateful to him.'

'He once told me the whole story. The whole astonishing story.'

'Did he, now? Stretching things a bit, wasn't he, if he did that?'

'He was very discreet. It has naturally—you'll forgive me —made me very interested in my new neighbour.'

'Kind of you, Sir John.' This came from Mr Povey with an irony that was impressively subdued. 'Do you know, I'd much like to meet Budgery again myself—and have him tell *me* the story?' Suddenly and unaccountably, Povey appeared genuinely agitated. 'You see, my own memories of it all are quite oddly confused. There was more to it, you must understand, than the shock of Charles's death. Arthur's death, I mean.' Povey broke off. 'Ah! You see how muddled I can get. But—since you've been told the whole medical history of the affair—you must have some idea why.' Povey's was now again a completely relaxed smile. 'There was more to it than just that dreadful accident—with a certain amount of subsequent privation and so forth thrown in. The fact is, I got a bit of a bang on the head myself. The consequences were rather astonishing for a time, as you justly observe.'

'You believed yourself to *be* Arthur?'

'Just that.' Povey made another pause. He had a good sense of timing. 'However, those Australian leeches—Budgery and his crowd—successfully bullied me out of it.'

'Brutally put, you were a bit mad?'

'Exactly so.' Povey, although he had raised his eyebrows, amicably concurred. 'And periods of confusion still turn up on me from time to time.'

'In which you again believe yourself to be Arthur?'

'Not very precisely that.' For the first time, Mr Povey had hesitated. 'But a great deal of amnesia, and that sort of thing.'

'Dear me! Most inconvenient.'

'Convenient, Sir John?' This time, Povey's eyebrows had really shot up.

'Inconvenient was the word I used.'

'Yes, of course. Damnably inconvenient, from time to time. This fellow Alcorne, for example, that they're making such a devil of a fuss about. There's a lot I don't clearly remember about him.'

'Ah, Alcorne.' Appleby had the wit to load with significance his repetition of this name. It was in fact entirely new to him.

'Yes, Alcorne. I had a lot to do with him a number of years ago. Naturally I remember *that*.' Povey laughed easily. 'We were partners, you know, and in a very big way. We were partners in several very large enterprises indeed. The enterprises they're now all going crazy about.'

'They?' Appleby said.

'All those chaps who are talking about fraud and conspiracy and God knows what. The chaps who are determined to bring me down.'

'They *have* brought you down, haven't they?'

'Yes, they have.' Mr Povey appeared to face it. 'Red ruin, without a doubt.'

'To the extent that your own wife, and that secretary of yours, and your whole staff for that matter, have pocketed what they can and bolted?'

'It looks like just that. But it's Jasper Alcorne I'm worried about—and particularly this business of not being able to remember things quite clearly. It might look bad.'

'Yes, Mr Povey, I agree. It might look *very* bad.' Appleby was feeling his way into this mysteriously sensitive area. 'The Alcorne affair was pretty bad at the time, wasn't it?'

'So I've gathered. I mean, yes—I do remember that. There we were, the two of us, as closely associated as could be. And *he* bolted, you know, just like that damned woman this morning, and with no end of securities and everything else. It turned out he'd been as crooked as they come. And I'd known nothing about it! We had the hell of a time putting a bold face on it. We had to sail pretty close to the wind ourselves, I don't mind telling you.'

'We?'

'Oh, myself and various close associates at that time. Assets had vanished in a big way. That kind of thing. Alcorne has never been seen since, and the scandal was forgotten about, more or less. But now, because of my present difficulties, those brutes in the City are all on to it again, digging away like mad. God knows what they may turn up.'

'I can tell you, Mr Povey.' Appleby suddenly sensed that the moment of truth was now very close indeed. He also felt that it might be hurried along by one or two thumping lies. 'I suppose you realize that this isn't—to be quite honest—any sort of social call?'

There was a moment's silence in the library of Brockholes. It seemed a very long moment. Appleby had time to wonder whether Povey *had* realized this pretty obvious fact or not. He felt no certainty in the matter. It depended on the truth about Povey's present mental state, and this was something entirely enigmatical. The man was deploying a good deal of cunning : there could be no doubt about that. Sometimes he seemed so baselessly confident of the sufficiency and success of all this guile that he must be judged as mad as a hatter. At other times he seemed entirely sane. Appleby told himself that one could be certain of only a single fact. The man with whom he was closeted was Arthur Povey. And Arthur Povey was very hazy about Jasper Alcorne for the simple reason that he had never got a grip on what appeared to have been a crucial episode in Charles Povey's career. Hence all this stuff about amnesia. It was as simple as that. And now Appleby went ahead.

'So let me be quite straight, Mr Povey. I'm a retired man now, but you know what my job has been. The unsolved mystery about your partner Alcorne lay on my desk for months. We had our own ideas about what might have happened to him—and I much doubt whether you can have *forgotten*'—Appleby put a vicious sarcasm into the uttering of this word—'the pretty nasty time we gave you. But we lacked proof. Well, all that has changed now. And— since it was all under my hand at the time—I've been asked to return and clear it up for good. That's why I'm at Brock- holes this morning, Mr Povey. And for no other reason at all.' As he produced this tissue of outrageous falsehoods Appleby leant forward threateningly and remembered to offer a ferocious scowl. No star of Scotland Yard in some television fantasy of criminal investigation could have been more magnificently intimidating. 'So now we'll have the truth, Charles Povey. And nothing but.' Perhaps for the first time in his life, Appleby had risen to a hideous snarl.

'I don't know what you're talking about!' Suddenly Povey sprang to his feet, trembling and as white as a sheet. He was a man horribly transformed.

'But indeed you do. How could this man Alcorne simply vanish—so utterly as to elude the search of every police force in the five continents? The very idea is nonsensical. And where did all those assets go? They went into your own pocket, Charles Povey. Because you were desperately in need of them. And I think it's true, isn't it'—Appleby's voice had dropped suddenly into a kind of spine-chilling caress—'that the Poveys always had a violent streak in them? Your brother Arthur for one. And certainly yourself.'

'It's untrue! It's ... it's—' Povey now had difficulty in managing articulate speech. 'I simply don't remember—'

'Rubbish.'

'I can prove—'

'It's no good, Charles Povey. Because the body—Alcorne's body—has now been found.'

'Alcorne murdered!' Povey's eyes had rounded in horror, and he was suddenly panting. 'But I have a way out! I've always had a way out! I told that bloody Butter so. You can't get me for killing this man Alcorne, or whatever's in your filthy head. I never set eyes on him.' Povey's voice rose to a scream. 'Because I'm not Charles Povey. I'm Arthur Povey. I've been ill. I tried hard to hang on to it that I'm Arthur. I've witnesses to that in Adelaide. I still try hard to be Arthur, but somehow it won't come. It was those doctors who made a lunatic of me. More and more, I don't know I'm Arthur any longer.' Povey collapsed again into his chair. 'I don't even know it now.'

XV

Sir John Appleby, although it would have been legitimate to describe him as a case-hardened man, was more than a little shaken by this latest effort on the part of his interlocutor. Roughly speaking, he was at a loss over how to estimate the genuineness, if any, of what could be called the Jekyll-and-Hyde aspect of the affair. He had already seen—it had come to him as he harangued Judith in the small hours—that Budgery's patient in the Adelaide hospital could be viewed as having insinuated himself into another man's shoes (and skin, for that matter) with astonishing ingenuity. He had manoeuvred his doctors into believing they were rescuing him from a bizarre delusion and restoring him to his true identity. One might call this deep enough, and Appleby had accorded it at once a species of generous professional admiration. It had never crossed his mind, however, that Arthur Povey's plan might have been deeper still; that he had managed, in a most notable degree, a further *tour de force* of what people nowadays liked to call contingency planning. There was an escape clause—a way out, as Povey had himself just expressed it—built into the plan from the start. The key word here—and this too Povey had used—was 'bullied'. The doctors had bullied him into a permanent, if mysteriously intermittent, pathological acceptance of his dead brother's identity. Morally speaking, Arthur Povey had maintained the right to be regarded as an innocent man. He might be booked for fame as a classical case-history, to be cited in textbooks as exemplifying the impenetrable strangeness of a human being's sense of his own

188

identity. He might well have to be committed to a mental hospital. But he couldn't be committed to gaol.

It was all, of course, the most unutterable nonsense. Appleby, as a rational man, felt something like sheer irritation as he contemplated its large absurdity. But not everybody remains successfully rational, even in a law-court. Take, for instance, one salient point. Arthur Povey had arrived in Adelaide minus—as his brother Charles was on record as being minus—the index finger of his left hand. Appleby imagined prosecuting counsel hammering this point home—and the jury, or at least a few obstinate members of a jury, saying to themselves *Yes, but*—and maintaining that the whole affair was too obscure and complicated to produce an adverse verdict upon.

But it wasn't any strength in Povey's case that was the point—at least the moral point—of the matter. Rather, it was its simple craziness. It was impossible to deny that the man was authentically deranged, and deranged in the most extraordinary way. *More and more, I don't know I'm Arthur any longer.* In any context of law, these words of Povey's were plain non-starters as any sort of exculpation. All along —the law would say—he had known, or at least intermittently he had known, his true identity. And nevertheless he had gone ahead being not the penniless Arthur but the affluent if embarrassed Charles——until the need for his 'way out' had overpoweringly come to him.

But this was only one view of that weird cry. Appleby's whole career had been built on backing his own sense of the truth of a situation until it was controverted by plain and acknowledged fact. And he now had a strong sense that Arthur Povey, obviously so abundantly given to systematic dishonesty and falsehood, had for once said an honest thing.

'I'm quite sane, you know,' Arthur Povey said. He had been silent for a full minute, and now he appeared almost calm.

189

He had been gazing thoughtfully at his own left hand, but now he raised his eyes and looked full at Appleby. 'I know who you are. I know you're a police officer. I know why you're here. I've always seen what suspicion might attach to me. We didn't get on very well—my brother and myself. And it was a lonely voyage of course, with tensions building up. We might well have quarrelled—I grant you that. But I didn't kill Arthur. He died just as I said. I escaped lightly from the accident—or seemed to. Only there was a blow that did something to my head.'

'You mean you didn't kill *Charles*? I believe that.'

'Charles?' It was like a man in pain that Arthur Povey uneasily moved his head. 'I don't understand you. Who do you think I am? What the devil do you mean?' Arthur Povey was silent again for a moment. 'You must be crazy,' he said.

Sir John Appleby, retired Commissioner of the Metropolitan Police, was aware of a sudden incongruous image floating somewhere inside his own head. It was of one of the delights of his childhood : a little wooden chalet out of which there bobbed, as the barometer rose or fell, now a little man and now a little woman. The notion of barometric pressure not having been within his intellectual grasp, it had been a mysterious phenomenon. Sometimes the little man and the little woman seemed to come and go with bewildering rapidity—a subjective impression, no doubt, occasioned by his being a good deal occupied in his nursery with a diversity of absorbing pursuits. And now the little man and the little woman were with him again.

What Arthur Povey had just produced—he told himself rather desperately—was simply his most superb turn yet. And it was far, far too good to be true. Only it *was* true. Appleby was in the veritable presence of Jekyll and Hyde. Only that didn't quite square with the facts of the case, since of these two famous fictional characters one had been a goody and the other a baddy. Whereas Charles and Arthur Povey could only be described as persons between whose moral worth, or lack of it, it would now be useless to attempt to discriminate. Appleby had solved their mystery, at least in a general way. What remained to tempt curiosity was a psychologist's affair—that, rather than a former policeman's. Arthur Povey had—but to a degree that remained obscure —been hoist with his own petard. Not, clearly, in a settled way, but rather with an intermittency which must make his life perpetually alarming.

And it was no business of *his*. This time, Appleby asserted this to himself seriously and after a moment's deliberate thought. It would be socially irresponsible, having discovered what he had discovered, not to pick up the telephone and call the police. But he had spent a long lifetime being socially responsible. Now, he rose to his feet, and called it a day.

'Mr Povey,' he said, 'you tell me you have been ill. You are still ill now, if my judgement isn't at fault. I'm going to see my family doctor. I shall ask him to call on you at once. I advise you to see him and confide in him. Meanwhile, forget that story about Alcorne having met a bad end. I know nothing about him. Good-bye.'

Appleby walked from the library and through the chilly hall; then, without pausing, he left Brockholes Abbey with no mind ever to return there. Rounding the house to regain the drive, however, he passed a line of garages. One remaining car was visible, and it was an uncommonly powerful one. He glanced at it briefly, grimly, and then drove away.

*   *   *

For some time Arthur Povey sat on in his deserted mansion, staring at a huge and empty fireplace. His head was troubling him. But, curiously enough, a headache usually signalled the lifting of those tiresome—and dreadfully dangerous—

confusions into which he now so often fell. He'd been having an increasingly hard time. *Both of him* had been having that.

He got up and mixed himself a drink. There was a cheerful side to the thing. He'd got rid of the horrible Pops, and of the treacherous Butter, and of all those low crooks battening on him as bogus domestic servants. And he'd foxed that policeman. He didn't quite remember *how* he'd foxed him, but he certainly had. Or had he? It didn't much matter. The infernal busybody was gone too.

He left the library and prowled through the big deserted house. He'd hated it as a boy, and he hated it now. And they'd wanted damn well to imprison him in the place! He was free at last.

Arthur Povey went up to his bedroom. He paused several times on the stairs to chuckle to himself. Only be clever enough, and you always get through. In the bedroom he pulled open drawers and packed a single suitcase. Just at the moment, it would be as well to travel light. Arthur—Charles, that was to say—despite his wealth had been quite good at that. Povey shoved aside a wardrobe, opened a safe concealed in the wall, and stuffed another suitcase with ten-pound notes. He stuffed it very full indeed, whistling to himself softly as he worked. There would be some sort of man-hunt, he supposed, but he wasn't afraid of that. He knew the sea (poor old Charles had never really known the sea) and that was an important point in favour of one who proposed to lead an elusive life. A *new* sort of elusive life—not one cooped up in a bloody morgue. He paused in his final preparations, and whistled a little more robustly. It had just dawned on him—for now his head was entirely clear—that for the rest of his days he wasn't going to be a Povey at all.

It was an immense release. He grabbed both suitcases, hurried out of the house, and drove triumphantly away in his big car.